Part of FOREVER

TAYLOR EPPERSON

Copy Editor - Kristen Hamilton

Proofreader - Chelsey Gordon

Cover Artist - Sam Palencia @inkandlaurel

I wrote this one for me, but as Taylor Swift said, "the story isn't mine anymore." Now, it's yours.

author's note

DEAR READER,

While this book is a love story, I can't promise a happy ending.

Please read these possible triggers before reading if you are someone who likes to be aware of certain content before reading:

- Cancer diagnosis
- Death
- Grief
- Parents who left
- Some swearing
- Religious/God themes

I share this list so that you can prepare yourself, or so you can read at a later date. Your mental health should always come first. So, please take care while reading. I did my best to handle these topics with care, and I hope that comes across while reading.

As always, I hope you enjoy this book when you pick it up.

Love, Taylor

prologue - tucker

JUST BEFORE I go out onstage, I kiss the tiny rose pendant on my necklace before tucking it back under my shirt. Then, I step out into the lights and can't help but grin.

The thrill is the same every time I step out onto the stage. I don't think it's a feeling I'll ever get over. Performing and the crowds going wild *for me*.

There is absolutely nothing like it.

And still, something is missing.

There's always something missing. As I walk across the stage, guitar in one hand and waving with the other, I try to push the feeling away.

I take my place at the front of the stage, sitting on the lone stool in front of the mic, and rest my guitar against my legs. I strum twice, making sure everything is still in tune.

"How's everybody doing tonight?" I ask into the mic, adding a little extra twang to my voice. The crowd cheers. There are phones out as far as I can see, pointed in my direction. It's surreal to be here.

I've been the opening act for bigger artists for the past few years.

This summer, though, I'm the main attraction, and I don't know if I'll ever be able to express what that means to me. How many twenty-one-year-olds can say they're living their dream?

I smile and take a deep breath. I can do this.

I glance up at the sky. It's clear tonight, but it's impossible to see the stars with all of the lights shining down on me. *Let's do this.*

"Thanks for coming out, y'all." More cheering. "Tonight is the last show of the ROSIE Tour, and I want to start with a song I don't normally sing." While I know this tour is named after my first (and currently only) album, *ROSIE,* I haven't sung this song yet.

I know the crowd will eat this up. My manager, Murphy, practically beamed when I told her my plans for the evening—and she's not an easy lady to please.

"Many of you know about my first single, 'Rosie.'" A hush of reverence falls over the crowd when I say the title—when I say her name. My heart thunders in my chest, and for a moment, the stadium in front of me disappears. All I see is her.

Her perfect smile, with full lips and auburn hair, pulled into a tight bun on her head. She's got an eyebrow raised at me, and her mouth opens as if she's about to say, "Well, are we going to do this or what?"

I blink away the image. As much as I love it, I can't exactly break down onstage the first time I ever sing her song live.

She'd hate that I call it her song, but it is. I think she'd also hate, just a little bit, that the reason I made it big was because of her; *is* because of her. Everything I have in this moment—*in my life*—is because of Rosie.

I play the first set of chords and swallow. It's time.

By the time I'm finished, I doubt there's a dry eye in the stadium. My face is wet as I stand and welcome the crowd to the tour once more, taking my next spot on the stage. The show must go on.

Life must go on.

Even if it breaks my heart.

three years earlier - rosie

1

THIS IS IT.

This is the moment that changes everything. Today's audition will determine what happens next in my life. If today goes well, my future will go exactly as I've hoped and planned since I was nine years old.

One more time, I think as I glance at the clock. I have exactly fifteen minutes until they call my name, until I audition in front of the panel of Paris Ballet Academy dancers. I've worked on drills with these dancers and the other ballerinas auditioning for a spot at PBA, but now it's time for the solo auditions. Thankfully, I have enough time to run through my routine one last time and have a few minutes to rest.

I push play on the stereo, grateful my mom thought to put five seconds of silence before the track started. It left just enough time for me to get to my place in the far corner of the room before the music started. The familiar notes hit my ears, and my body reacts instantly.

I was born to be a ballerina.

Everyone who watches me dance says that. It feels like the music and I are melded together so closely that everyone else sees it coming to life. It's as if the melody and my body have become one. Dancing is as natural as breathing for me.

This is it.

I'm breathing hard when the song ends. My muscles scream in pain as I walk over to my bag and pull out my phone. I've been pushing my body to its limit this week. Mom would be proud. She'd also told me to turn off my phone before coming into the training room because she didn't want me to have any distractions. I glance over my shoulder toward the door, half expecting her to come waltzing through even though I know she's not allowed to see me until after my audition. She has to stay in the lobby with all of the other parents.

I probably shouldn't turn it on.

I sink onto the floor, giving my tattered feet a break. At this point, my torn-up feet are just a hazard from being a ballerina and pointe dancer.

What I need is a nice long bath and a break. While I can probably soak in the tub this afternoon, I don't think I'll get a break from dancing anytime soon. Not that I want one; dancing is in my blood. It's the only thing that makes me feel alive.

I glance around the empty space one more time as I switch my phone on. My belly flips in this simple act of rebellion. I just need a distraction. At least that's what I tell myself. I feel ready and confident that I am going to kill this part of the audition, but I'm still a ball of nerves. The butterflies remind me of how I feel before every performance or competition. They won't go away until I get out on the floor, in front of the panel, and dance.

Until then, I welcome the opportunity to focus on something —anything—else... My phone vibrates with notifications as the door to the room opens, and I throw my phone back into my bag. I try to sit as though I'm just sitting, and not like I'm about to get caught looking at my phone before the biggest audition of my life.

But it's not my mom; it's Elena, another ballerina auditioning for PBA that I just met two days ago.

"Could I run through my routine in here?" she asks nervously. "The stereo in my practice room doesn't work."

"Sure." I smile at her. She might be my competition, but she's good. I'd bet that she and I both make it into the academy. They only take six new dancers each year, and there are fifty of us in this studio right now, either warming up, practicing, or auditioning.

Elena smiles in relief. "Thanks." She walks over to the stereo and plugs her phone in. I watch as she gets started.

Mom has told me a thousand times not to get too close to the other girls here. She told me it's best not to have friends in the dance world because it gets too messy when you make a team and they don't, or vice versa. Mom probably would have told Elena no. But I'm not Mom—something I'm grateful for.

I love her as my mom, but as a dance coach, she's a little intense. And I'd rather have friends. Elena seems like a good one.

I close my eyes, listening to the music while Elena runs through her routine. I should stretch so my muscles aren't tight when they come to get me for my audition, but I don't want to move. I imagine the pirouettes and leaps I will do as the music crescendos.

The music stops, and I stand.

"Thanks again." Elena grabs her phone and walks toward me, hugging me. "Good luck on your audition. I'd love to see you in Paris next year if we both make it. Maybe we could room together."

I smile. "I'd like that."

She leaves, and I'm left alone with my thoughts. I don't have enough time to check the texts that came through as I turned my phone on, so they'll just have to wait until later.

I look at myself in the mirror. Today is January 3rd, the day I've been training for every day for the past three years. This audition means everything. My future depends on me dancing my best today, and I will be excellent.

The door opens.

"Rosie Dillon?" A small woman with graying hair peeks into the room. "They're ready for you." I smile at myself in the mirror and stand a little taller as I follow her out of the room and down the hall.

I am Rosie Dillon, daughter of Catherine Dillon, and I am the best ballerina on the West Coast.

The audition room is only slightly larger than my rehearsal space. The panel sits at a narrow table in front of the mirror; there are three women and one man watching as I walk across the room. A small *X* in the middle of the floor marks where I'm meant to stand.

"Rosie Dillon," the man says, smiling. This is David Caron. He trained my mother and observed many of my sessions last summer, when I went to Paris for a boot camp, as well as the group auditions over the last two days. "What a pleasure to see you again."

I nod, Mom's words echoing inside my head. *Do not speak until they ask you a question.*

"Oh, this is Catherine's girl?"

I don't recognize the woman on the right as she takes me in again. She smiles this time, and I'm sure she sees Mom in parts of my features. I look more like my dad, but my delicate frame resembles my mother's.

The middle woman, Babette Moss, who's been in the ballet world for over fifty years, squints at me. "Could you tell us more about yourself and why you've chosen to audition for the Paris institution?"

I nod and then say the words I've practiced a hundred times, hoping they don't come out sounding rehearsed. "I'm Rosie Dillon. I've been dancing since I was five. I stopped dancing when I was seven and was diagnosed with cancer. After treatment, when

I was almost nine, I started training again. I'll have been in remission for nine years next month." I smile at this part; it's been almost nine years that I've been cancer-free. I continue, "I chose Paris first because it is where my mother was professionally trained. I am choosing Paris now because it is the best academy in the world, and I want to dance with the best."

Everyone smiles at me, and the woman on the right makes a note. I know I've said exactly what they want to hear. Mom coached me on what to say. A little bit of my sob story about how I had to take off years of training, but have now come back, even better than I was before.

"You may take your place, then the music will begin," Babette tells me. I nod and head to the far right corner of the room. Just as it did in the practice room, as soon as the music starts, everything else fades away as it becomes a part of me, and I tell a story through dance.

2

"HOW DID IT GO?" Mom asks only once we're in the car, heading away from the studio. She hates talking about dance or how my personal auditions went in front of anyone else, because she believes they would be held in a gym and not a private studio if they were meant to be public.

I'm still on a high from my audition and can't help but grin. "It was flawless."

She nods in approval, as if she expected nothing less. I stare out the window, taking in the buildings of LA. It's not a city I love. I personally crave the salty air and ocean breeze that comes from living in a beach city, but today, Los Angeles is full of promise and the beginning of my future. It is my friend today, even with the early rush hour traffic.

"Remember," Mom says, and I catch myself groaning inwardly. A lecture already? I just finished the best audition of my life. Can't we just enjoy that for a moment? "Even though the audition is over, we're not done training. You'll still need to be at the studio every day after school."

"I know." I sigh, even though I might have secretly been hoping for a tiny break, even just a few days. I love ballet, but having Mom be a part of that world sometimes makes it a little too intense. Up until this year, she's been my coach. This year, though, she's paying an arm and a leg for Maria Lilleth to coach me privately so that I will be ready for Paris. Mom still helps on the side, but Maria is the one I listen to most, even though Mom acts more like a coach than a mom most of the time.

I smile, thinking of Maria. She called me this morning to wish me luck and to remind me that to be the best, I had to act like I was the best. She is about to have a baby and is currently on bed rest— or on the couch in her studio.

"I'm going to text Maria and tell her how it went," I say as I slide my phone out.

It was flawless.

I use the same words I used to tell my mother, because it was flawless. There's no other word for it. She texts back moments later.

MARIA LILLETH

Wonderful. We'll talk tomorrow about our new training plan. Now that you've auditioned, we've got to get you ready to dance there.

These words, coming from Maria and not Mom, make me smile. I look at my phone again, opening the texts I didn't read earlier.

The Four Musketeers Group Chat:

GRACE

You're going to do great, Rosie!

NATHAN

Go rock it, Sis!

Also, tell Mom that we're out of apples.

TUCKER

What do apples have to do with the audition?

GOOD LUCK ROSIE!! YOU'RE GOING TO DO
AMAZING.

TUCKER (OUT OF GROUP CHAT)

Seriously, you'll do great. I can't wait to hear
how it goes :)

I flush as I read the last text from Tucker. We've been good friends since he moved to California three years ago, during our freshman year, to be a country singer. He's cute, but not the type of guy my mom wants me to date. He's Grace's cousin and moved in with her family while his mom stayed in Tennessee for work. He originally moved because he had a record deal lined up, which fell through three weeks later. But he stayed, because even though country music is his thing, he feels like LA is the place for him to make it in the music world. Plus, his dad isn't here. I shake thoughts of his strained relationship with his father out of my head and instead remember the first time I met him.

We had an instant friendship after what Grace calls a 'meet-cute.' I think she's been hoping we'd get together the whole time we've known each other. I won't lie; there is something between us, but for now, we're just friends. That's all we can be while Mom has a say in my life, and she's got the final say in everything.

I frown when I realize there's no good luck text from Shawn, the guy my mom wants me to date. A flash of guilt rushes through me because of the pleasure I felt when I read Tucker's texts. I shouldn't be feeling that way about another guy, right? Even if I don't have a relationship with Shawn. I've known him nearly all my life, and Mom thinks we're destined to be together. Our dads are good friends, and at the beginning of our senior year, our moms started conspiring to get us to date. They talk on and on for hours and hours about how great he is and how he'll be going to Yale in the fall to be a doctor, and I should date him because he'll be dedicated to school and work while I have a dance career. Plus, she brought up that I'd had a crush on him when we were younger.

She doesn't care that I don't like him like that. Not anymore.

When I mentioned that after the Christmas dance, she told me that I needed to start thinking about my future after dance because I won't be able to dance forever. But that's not something I ever want to think about.

I shake all the thoughts away and turn my phone over without texting anyone back. I cannot afford to be distracted, especially not by my mom's plans or by Tucker. He's the reason why I told my mom I'd try dating Shawn in the first place. It was the perfect proposition. Shawn wanted to make his real crush, Libby, jealous, and I didn't want to date Tucker. I can't date him.

I sigh. I would actually love to date him, even though I have no intention of telling him that. He's the person who makes me laugh the most, and he understands (on some level) my dedication to dance and knows why today is so important to me. He gets me on a level no one else does, and I get him the same way. But, as much as I want to hold his hand every now and then, and even if I wonder if kissing him is as great as it was last summer when we'd had our first and only kiss, Tucker Bensen is not an option.

Mom had made that clear as soon as he'd moved in.

Which probably made me like him even more.

"No boys," she had said one afternoon after class.

"What?" I asked, confused at what she was referring to, as I drank from my water bottle, still going through the routine in my mind.

"I know Erin's nephew just moved in. She said that the two of you hit it off the other day at his welcoming party. But you know the rules."

"Mom," I'd groaned, "it's not like that. We're just friends." Because at that point, of course that's all we were. We were still practically strangers. Yes, I thought he was cute, but I was married to ballet already, even at fourteen. I wouldn't let anything or anyone stop me from getting into the Paris Ballet Academy.

Mom looked at me with that stern and serious look then—it was the look she gave dancers in the studio often. "No boys, no distractions," she said firmly.

I nodded. "No boys, no distractions."

When it became apparent to nearly everyone that Tucker and I connected on a level no one could have ever guessed, I tried to step back from the flirting and the long glances for the sake of all involved. But even if I hadn't had dance to focus on, I think I would have cut back anyway. We became better friends, and eventually, I didn't have to remind myself that *we're just friends* every time we were together. I didn't want to mess up our friendship.

Until he kissed me on the Fourth of July last year during the firework show.

Immediately, I wanted him to do it again. And just as immediately, I knew I had to make it stop. Now, we're back to being friends and pretending like it never happened. I went to Paris for the last half of summer and came back to Mom's plan for me to date Shawn. But he and I aren't interested in each other, even if we flirt occasionally to make our moms think otherwise. I don't like him, and he doesn't like me. But Mom could tell I was starting to fall for Tucker, so she intervened. Just like she always does.

My phone vibrates in my hands, pulling me out of my thoughts.

NATHAN

Are you coming to the bonfire with us tonight?

I flip my phone over, unsure of my answer. Part of me really wants to say no. It's a Monday night, and school starts tomorrow, so I'd much rather spend a few hours in the studio and go to bed before ten. But it's my senior year, and tomorrow, I start my last semester of high school, which means I can finally go to the senior bonfire with my friends.

"So," I say, broaching the subject with my mom because her answer is always no unless it's a movie night or a party at Grace's house, "the senior bonfire is tonight, and Nathan and Grace are going, and I want to go with them."

The words tumble out, and my stomach flips. What if she says no? I hate that I feel small as I say these words, like she has so much power over me that I've made myself smaller so that it won't hurt nearly as much when the crushing blow comes. She doesn't treat Nathan this way, only me. Her little 'prodigy', even if that's not what I ever wanted to become.

"Hmm?" Mom asks, glancing away from the stopped traffic to look at me. Why can't she ever listen when I talk?

"The bonfire? Tonight. Can I go with them?"

"Will Tucker be there?" she asks, and I clench my teeth.

"I don't know," I tell her honestly. "But it doesn't matter since everything with Shawn is going well."

She frowns. "Will he be there?" she asks. She's not thrilled that he and I have only gone on two dates since the summer. She wants me to try harder to make him my boyfriend, but there's only one guy I'm interested in, and it's the only one she doesn't want me to date. Although I used to have a crush on Shawn, that was before I got to know him better.

"No, he's flying in tonight from Colorado. Skiing, remember?"

She nods, as if she only sort of remembers this.

I'm afraid she'll tell me no; that since he won't be at the bonfire, she won't let me go.

"Fine," she says, and my heart leaps—slightly.

Dare I hope I heard her correctly? "Really?"

"Really," she answers. "But you both have to be home by ten at the latest. It is a school night."

"Thanks, Mom," I say, turning my phone over.

YES. And Mom said yes since I finally
asked her.

NATHAN

Good call on waiting till after your audition to
ask her.

That was partly Tucker's idea. He suggested I
wait until she wasn't focused on the audition to
ask her. Is he coming?

NATHAN

Good man. And yes, he'll be there.

I swallow, glancing at Mom. She'll get worried if she knows he's coming, but I'm not about to tell her and give her a reason to change her mind. She gets funny when Tucker is concerned. She's worried that he's too much like my dad and that I'm going to fall head over heels for him and ruin my career by having kids too soon, which is what happened to her.

My parents' love story is one that I loved hearing as a child. Dad would sit us down and share how, during their senior year of high school, his parents moved from Laguna Beach down to San Clemente, a thirty-minute drive that he was convinced would ruin his life. On his first day, he met Mom, and he knew that was it; he was head over heels for a girl he didn't even know yet.

From the way they tell it, they fell in love fast, and he followed her to Paris, declaring he could paint anywhere, which was true. He worked in the Louvre at the front desk as she danced the days away. He proposed when they were nineteen and they were married three months later. By twenty-two, she had twins on the way, and her professional dance career was over. Not because she was now a mother, but because Nathan and I broke her pelvis during the first part of delivery before it turned into an emergency C-section.

Her life is the reason she has all these strict rules about boys, because she wants for me what she never got, even though I know she loves Dad and she loves us. I think part of her regrets having kids when she did because she didn't get to finish her dream. It's why she gets to choose who I date. Guys who have "real potential," as she says. Which tells me she doesn't know Shawn very well because he has as much potential as a golden retriever. He's a nice guy, but I'm pretty sure he plans on surfing instead of going to college like his parents think.

But I could be with Tucker now. The thought enters my mind so quickly that I drop my phone, startled. *The audition is over. Why not have some fun with him before school ends? It could be the end of senior year/summer romance you've always wanted.*

The thought makes me smile, but then I shake my head. I don't want to ruin our friendship; I have to protect that at all costs. If we get together, there's a risk we will come out on the other end not as friends, and I don't know if I can take that risk.

journal entries from freshman year

NOVEMBER 17TH

Dear Journal,

Okay. Wow. I've never actually written that before. I guess I'm not sure how to start a new journal, even though I've done it a million times.

This one, though, is just in a random notebook that looks like all of my school notebooks so Mom won't think to look at it. I think.

She's nosy and reads my other journal. She pretends she doesn't, but she knows things I only write in there… and that's annoying and makes me mad. I asked her about it once, but she denied it. Anyway. Not the point of why I'm writing today.

Tonight, Grace threw a party.

I can't believe we're finally freshmen and she's already throwing parties.

And that people actually came!

Her party was for her cousin, Tucker, who just moved to town. I guess he's some singer or something and wanted to come here to be closer to LA. I think she said he had a record deal (is that even what it's called?) but I was too nervous to ask him about it. Not that I even talked to him much.

Me and Nathan went to Grace's early after she sent a text saying she was baking. BAKING!! Like, can you imagine her baking anything? Grace is a great writer who loves all things Disney and Disneyland related (she'd really love to be Mulan in all the parades and stuff one day) but she is NOT a baker. We got there right as she dumped a cup of sugar into the bowl.

She just laughed and said she didn't know she actually needed to use the recipe.

Typical Grace.

But the cupcakes were saved, thanks to me and Nathan.

Grace kept talking about her cousin, who I guess at that point was just hiding in his room—she said he was unpacking, but I think he was hiding. Grace can be intense sometimes. I love her, but still, she'll smother you with love. I was curious though. I may have stalked him on Instagram to see if I could find out more about him. The most recent picture Grace had was a picture from when they were seven. IG wasn't super helpful though; his profile picture is just a shadow of him and he mostly posts pictures of his guitar.

Why do I feel like I need to share my entire life story up to this point before I go on? Like, yes, it's a new journal, but who exactly do I think will be reading this???? NO ONE, HOPEFULLY.

Anyway. I'm a dancer. A good dancer. I've been working so, so hard. Which is why Mom has a rule about no boys.

And I'm 14. It really hasn't been a problem before. I've had crushes, but nothing major.

Then I saw Tucker tonight.

I didn't even really meet him. Gosh, I think I'm blushing just writing about it. I'm so embarrassed. WHY AM I WRITING ABOUT THIS?? It's not even a big deal.

We didn't even say HELLO!

After we finished making the cupcakes, I went downstairs to where a Disney movie was playing (when is one not *playing at Grace's house?) and listened to my competition routine music on my headphones for a while, until people started showing up.*

Grace came down with the cupcakes, then Nathan came down with a few of his friends. I have the two of them, they're my two best friends (and Nathan is my twin sooo...) but I sometimes forget that in the real world, when it's not just us, I just have dance, but they are friends with a lot of people.

Wow, I keep going off on tangents. I am way too tired for this. Anyway. Do I say anyway a lot? Anyway (ugh), Nathan brought me a cupcake, and I'd just taken a freakishly huge bite when Tucker appeared at the bottom of the stairs.

I knew it was him immediately because he looks just like Grace's mom, which makes sense, since she and his mom are twins... (how is it that I'm a twin and my best friend's mom is a twin? Do most people in real life know that many twins?) (focus Rosie)

Tucker is tall, way taller than I expected. Probably close to six feet. He's got blue eyes and I think blondish, brownish hair; it was hard to tell since he was wearing a gray baseball cap, backwards.

Grace was making the rounds with him and introducing him to everyone. Before they could get to me, her mom yelled from upstairs about a batch of cookies burning, so Grace ran up the stairs.

He sat on the couch opposite me, talking with Nathan. Then he looked up at me.

His eyes were (are) so blue, like the ocean on a clear morning. I love that color so much, and they were just looking at me.

I think I gave a sort of smile. Then, I shoved the rest of the cupcake in my mouth. WHY AM I LIKE THIS?

Once I swallowed (finally) I looked up, and Tucker was still looking at me. Super embarrassing.

But wanna know what's even more embarrassing (whoever this imaginary person is that I'm writing to...)

When we got home, I followed him on Instagram. I mean, his account isn't private and he doesn't have that many followers, but I still followed him. Then I deleted the app before I could change my mind.

I have no idea why I am the way I am. I didn't even talk to the guy and I still feel so awkward. I'm so glad tomorrow is the rehearsal for our Christmas concert in a few weeks, so I can just dance all day and not think about him.

And how blue his eyes are.

Or how he watched me stuff my face with a cupcake (why couldn't I just take normal bites like a normal person?????)

Okay.

I'm going to bed.

I will not redownload Instagram. I will not. I will not. I will not.

Love, Rosie

3

"WE'RE HERE," Nathan yells from the studio lobby just as I turn off the music. Now that I'm finished with my audition, I can work on my two solos for the spring concert in a few months and the few class routines I have for my pointe class. When we got back from the audition, I had Mom drop me off here, even though I knew Nathan and Grace would pick me up soon. So much for soaking in a warm bath. Adrenaline was still pumping through my body from the audition, and I couldn't sit at home and wait for my friends to be ready. So, I came to dance.

"Just a sec," I call to my brother. The studio is small, so I know he heard me. I slip some black leggings on over my tights and pull my blue, faux cashmere sweater over my head. I glance at myself in the mirror. My hair is in a messy bun, and my face is red from all the dancing. *It'll have to do.* Tonight is just another night that I'll look like I came from rehearsal, which is technically true.

"There you are." I spin in surprise at the voice. Tucker is leaning against the doorway of the small room with his hands in the pockets of his worn jeans.

"Tucker," I say, slightly breathless, and he gives me that half-smile that makes my heart do funny flips. "I didn't know you were coming." *Lie*. Nathan told me he would be here earlier.

He steps toward me. "Everyone's waiting in the car." His words should make me feel bad because I promised I'd be ready to go when they arrived. Grace hates to be late to things, even when they're informal. But his easy smile makes it seem like he doesn't have a care in the world about rushing anywhere.

"How did your audition go?" he asks.

I grab my bag and follow him down the narrow hallway to the main entrance, flipping off the lights as we go. "It was incredible," I say. "I did well, and they loved it from what I could see."

It sounds cocky, even to me, but he grins at me. "I knew you'd do great."

"Thanks," I say as we head outside into the cool winter air. Living in a beach city in the middle of winter is weird. At least, that's what Tucker always tells us. There's never any snow; lately, there's rarely even rain. What we call freezing is what most Americans would probably wear a thin jacket for— another thing he often reminds us of. I shiver in the slight breeze, grateful I asked my brother to grab my coat on his way. Even by the fire, tonight will be cold.

Waiting in the parking lot is a pale green van, windows down and music blasting. Tucker cringes when we step outside.

"Leo's having the time of his life." Nathan laughs as we approach the minivan. Leo, Grace's boyfriend of two months, thinks it makes him cooler to listen to rap while he drives his mother's minivan, the only car we can all fit in without having our parents drive us.

"I have nothing against rap," Tucker says, wincing as Leo turns the music up. "It just doesn't make his van any cooler."

I can't help but laugh as I slide the door open. Leo turns the music down and we climb into the old van.

"Finally," Grace says, but grins from the front seat. "We're going to have so much fun tonight."

I smile back at her, grateful that the first thing she said was not about dancing. I climb into the backseat, Tucker following me, and Nathan slides the door shut after he's seated in the middle of the van.

"Rosie," Grace says, "how did your audition go?"

I smile. I can't help it. "It was practically perfect," I say, and she grins at me. Grace has been my best friend since we were babies. I guess that's what happens when your moms grow up as best friends. She's petite and looks flawless nearly all the time. Grace did ballet for a while, but then found her true love in soccer.

"Yay!" Grace claps, and my smile widens. "I'm so glad it went so well. I can't wait to hear what they say!"

"You'll get in." Tucker smiles at me, and Grace claps again.

"Just don't forget about me when you're famous," she says, and I can't hold back my grin.

"I could never."

"Promise you'll be around more now that your audition is over?" she asks, and for a moment, I freeze.

"I promise I won't dance as much now that my audition is over," I say, but I know the words are hollow. I know I say it a lot, but ballet *really is* everything to me. It's the one thing I'm good at —the only thing that really means anything to me. I'm not going to stop dancing for hours every day simply because my audition is over. That would feel like a waste. I have to keep training. Maybe not as hard as I did before my audition, but I'll still be in the studio every day.

Most people think ballet comes naturally to me, especially those within the ballet world, because of who my mom is and the dancer she was. But I started later than most ballerinas because Dad wanted to make sure it was my choice to dance. When you start training to be a ballerina at age five instead of age three, you're already two years behind. Then, when I got sick, that put me further behind. I have to work hard every single day if I'm going to be the best. I don't mind putting in all the extra hours. I dance until

I bleed because this is what I want more than anything. I want to dance with the Paris Ballet Academy, and I want to be remembered.

"There are more important things than being famous and remembered," Grace says as if reading my mind.

"I know," I say, even though I don't believe it for a second. There are billions of people on the planet. Who doesn't want to be remembered? Eager for a topic change because I don't want to make any more promises we all know I won't keep, I turn to Tucker. "Any word yet?"

He's been waiting all week to hear back from his manager, Murphy, about a possible record deal or tour opening. "Nothing yet." He shakes his head. "These things take time."

"But she promised she'd have news this week," I say. I notice that even though he's playing it off, he's not okay about it. I can see in his eyes that he wishes he had some news, good or bad.

"That's Murphy for ya," he says with a half-shrug, like he's trying to convince himself that it really is no big deal, then smiles at me. "She did text earlier saying she heard back from one of the recording studios. I guess they like my stuff, but they want to change all the lyrics of my song, so it feels like they don't like my stuff. I don't know. She said I could think about it, but I know there's gonna be someone who wants me *and* my songs, so I think I'm gonna wait."

"That's really awesome," I say, "I mean, not the part about them wanting to change your lyrics, but you're on the radar. Someone's gonna pick you up." I nudge his knee with mine, hoping to give him a little boost. He's going to make it big some day, he's got to believe that.

He winks. "Thanks for your confidence, darlin'."

My cheeks grow warm. He's called me that from the beginning. I thought it was cute and charming since he came from Nashville. It's still charming, but lately, it's been making me all warm inside when he says it. Even though I lie to myself every day about not wanting to be with him, I do, and the way he's always flirting with me and teasing me doesn't help.

Then he says, "But hey, this time next year, I'll be on tour, and you'll be in Paris."

I smile. It's another great thing about being friends with him. While Grace thinks I dance too much, he gets it—at least on some level.

We've both got big dreams that any average parent would try to dissuade and push us down a more normal or stable path, but not ours. My parents and his mom are all big dreamers. Even with his dad being who he is—one of the most famous country singers of our time and also the man who left behind his wife and child to sing—his mom still encourages him to do what he wants to do, which happens to be singing country music.

Neither of us has a backup plan. It's Paris or nothing. It's making it big or nothing.

I want to dance.

He wants to sing.

"It'll be amazing," I say, and then we fall into a comfortable silence, chiming in occasionally to whatever Grace and Nathan are talking about next. Leo drives, singing along to every song on the radio. I smile, but I can't help but feel that familiar tug that makes me wish I was still dancing in the studio.

My brother disappears almost as soon as we get to the beach, calling out to us that he'll catch up with us later, but that he wants to meet up with his new boyfriend first. Grace suggests we head over to the fire, which I readily agree with because the slight ocean breeze makes me shiver.

She grabs Leo's hand and we follow them across the dark

beach; when they stop to talk to one of Leo's surfing buddies, we continue to the fire.

"Looks like it's just you and me," Tucker says. He's got his hands in the front pockets of his jeans again, and my heart speeds up as I look at him. I think about Shawn as I scan the beach, all too aware of how closely Tucker stands by me. Even if Shawn could have come tonight, I probably still would have come with my friends and he would have shown up with his. That usually happens when my mom forces me to attend an event with him.

"Wanna sit?" I ask and wring my hands together, trying to ease my nerves about being alone with him.

It's not like we've never been alone before. But there's an energy between us that feels different tonight. It's felt like this since the end of last school year when we somehow became more than friends after he went to prom with someone else. It's like that date made him realize he wanted to be with me. I'd been mostly keeping my feelings pushed down up until that point. We started flirting then, and he gave me the perfect first kiss on the Fourth of July, but then I went to Paris, and everything changed. Maybe it's because my audition is over. Maybe I could be with him for real if I wanted to now. But I don't want to ruin our friendship. I'm not ready to mess up our balance of being friends who flirt sometimes, because if something went wrong, I'd lose one of my best friends. At least, that's what I keep telling myself.

"Sure," he says, and I follow him to the benches surrounding the huge fire. The sun has set, and the sky is now a deep purple. My classmates are everywhere, most of them carrying red cups that are probably full of cheap beer.

"So this is the big senior bonfire." He gestures around us, taking it all in. "And your mom let you come?" he asks as we sit on a large log near the fire.

My leg brushes against his, but neither of us moves away from the other. I wish it didn't feel so comfortable being here with him, but I can't help how I feel when I'm around him; it's like my rational brain decides to quit. At least I can somewhat keep up with the small talk.

"Yeah." I watch the flames, trying to get Mom's face out of my mind as I look down at my hands. "Mom is dedicated to me becoming a great dancer, and, I mean, I am too. But she has me practicing at five most mornings, so going out late isn't usually an option."

"But tonight?"

I glance at him as he asks me this, and when his blue eyes meet mine, I feel that familiar lurch in my stomach—the one that makes me want to be more than friends with him, even if that's not a good idea.

"My audition was this morning, so I don't really need to be practicing tonight." I watch the red and orange flames; that same flicker of guilt that I felt in the car flashes through me again—that even though my audition is over, I should still be dancing. Training. Doing something to make sure I'm actually ready to dance in Paris if I get in.

"Well, I'm glad she said yes. We've all been a bit worried about you. Grace says you've become obsessed with perfecting your routine."

"I have not." The words come out snappy, but I don't take them back and apologize. "Not that it matters. My audition is done."

He lifts his hands in surrender. "Hey, just repeating what she said. But I do think you could use a break, you look exhausted."

I look at him then, because I *have* been feeling more tired than usual. Mom chalked it up to having four-hour rehearsals most days after school, but there's a feeling in my gut that makes me wonder if it's something more. Like all the times before, though, I brush the feeling aside. I've been tired because I've been practicing so much. "I've been working extra hard since I got back from Paris. This audition determines everything about my future."

His jaw tightens at the mention of my Paris trip last summer, but a split second later, the tension is gone—possibly imagined—and he gives me his famous half-smile. "I don't think that one moment could have such a powerful impact on your future."

I let out a slow breath. He doesn't understand. "It does."

"I mean, don't get me wrong"—he bumps my knee with his—"I feel that same way every time I send in a song to a different record company, but it goes away. Because I know that even if it's not this one, maybe it'll be the next one. I just keep trying."

"It's not like that with ballet," I tell him, pulling on my fingers, which I've noticed I do every time I start thinking about the possibility of not dancing in Paris. "If I want to get into the Paris Academy, this is my only shot. They rarely take students who don't make it on the first try."

He whistles. "Sounds rough."

"It is," I say, and we fall into a silence that makes me wish we were still talking, because now I'm feeling jittery about not dancing, even though my audition is over.

Tucker reaches across my lap and separates my anxious hands, threading his fingers through mine. "I know you did great," he tells me, squeezing my hand. When he pulls away a second later, the loss of heat is all I feel.

"Hey, Rosie!"

The bubble I always find myself in when he is around pops as I see Meg, Shawn's younger sister, walking toward us. This might be the *senior* bonfire, but I forgot that most of the school shows up.

"Meg. Hi," I say too brightly, and she gives me a weird look. I'm thankful that the sun has set, so the chances of her seeing how red my cheeks are are slim.

"You still coming to dinner on Sunday?" she asks, and I watch as her eyes move between Tucker and me. Even before Mom thought Shawn would make a perfect boyfriend for me, since our families have been kind of close all my life. We occasionally do dinner's at each others houses. Which is fine, but not my favorite. I'd rather be dancing or with my friends.

But, that's why pretending to be interested in him made sense logically. He is trying to make a girl jealous, and I'm trying not to fall harder than I already have for Tucker. My dad can see right through us, though. He knows this isn't what I want, but he hasn't said anything to me, and since Mom hasn't asked me about it, I assume he's kept to himself what he knows—or thinks he knows.

"Probably." I'm grateful that my voice sounds normal now. "My mom said she's going to make her famous chocolate cheesecake."

Meg smiles at me, and from down the beach, one of her friends calls her name. "Awesome! I've got to go, I just wanted to say hi."

"Have fun tonight," I tell her.

"You too," she says, glancing between the two of us again before heading off. With Meg gone, Tucker and I fall into an awkward silence again. I intentionally stare at the fire for a few minutes before I look at him. Things have been weird between us ever since I got back from Paris, and I miss how things used to be.

"Wanna dance?" I blurt, startling both of us.

"What?" he asks.

I point to the people I noticed dancing by the water when we arrived. It's too cold to swim, but some boys pull the girls close to the water, trying to hear them squeal.

"Want to dance?" I ask breathlessly, as if I'll lose my nerve if I don't. "With me?"

"Won't Shawn mind?"

I shrug. "Who's he to tell me I can't dance with one of my best friends? Plus, sitting here is making my mind only think about my audition which is stressing me out because I can't change anything, and I know dancing will help, especially if it's not the kind of dancing I normally do. Especially if it's with you." All the words tumble out in a rush. I need to tell him the truth about how my mom wants me to date Shawn, not me, but I can't bring myself to say the words.

I can't read him, even though I'm watching the light of the fire skirt across his face.

I stand up and hold out a hand. "I don't care what he thinks. I want to dance with you."

He looks torn for a moment before he jumps up and reaches for my hand. "Let's do it." He doesn't let go as we walk across the sand, and right now, I don't care if anyone sees.

There's loud music from a portable speaker when we get to where the people are dancing. I laugh as Tucker throws his arms up in the air and starts jumping up and down.

The rest of the night, we're like this; a little out of breath, touching each other too much for people who are just friends and for someone who's supposed to like someone else. But part of me loves the thrill and fireworks of it all. I love watching his eyes light up when a song he likes starts playing, and how he keeps purposely bumping into me during fast songs and holding me close during the slow ones.

"I'm really glad we're friends," I say as he pulls me into him as "I'll Be" starts playing from the speaker.

"Me too." He breathes against me. My head settles against his chest. He's got one hand on my lower back, the other wrapped around my hand, and I listen to his heartbeat and breathe in the salty air.

Grace finds us after that, saying it's time to go, and we're both quiet the whole way home. I can't help but wonder what he's thinking about.

Later, after I get upstairs, I finally pull out my phone. I have three texts from Tucker. Two were from earlier in the evening, and one was from just a few minutes ago.

TUCKER

We're here.

NVM, I'll just come in to get you.

10:35 PM

"I Belong" by Tyler Hilton

I pull up the song on Spotify and close my eyes while I listen, my heart beating wildly. The last time he sent me a song was back in May of last year. It's been nine months, and he's still sharing his feelings through songs. My heart nearly stops as I realize his feelings are exactly the same as they've always been.

And so are mine.

4

"DON'T FORGET, we have a math quiz on Friday, so our next class will be our review day," Mrs. Adams says from the front of the room, switching off her overhead projector.

She's been a teacher at the school for over thirty years, and while most teachers have adjusted their teaching methods to newer technology, Mrs. Adams, who's probably in her mid-seventies, still uses an overhead projector. I didn't even know what that was until I showed up to my first pre-calc class at the beginning of the school year.

Even though Mrs. Adams is a bit old-school, she's my favorite teacher this year. She loves teaching, which is why she still does it. But it might also be that we have the world's best math class.

There are Ellie and Simon, who never fail to make us laugh at least once in every class. Grace sits next to me, and Tucker sits behind us. While that's about where my friend group ends, Grace is friends with almost everyone in the class, and they're all friends with each other, too. We threw a surprise Christmas party with a white elephant exchange one day, only to celebrate Hanukkah the next day in class because Mrs. Adams is Jewish.

She actually cried because it made her day.

"I am not looking forward to Friday," I groan as the final bell rings. I then slip my notebook into my backpack.

"Why?" Grace asks, pulling out a Tootsie Pop from her bag. "Want one?"

"No thanks," I tell her. "And I'm not looking forward to Friday because we have that math quiz. Plus it's my yearly cancer checkup."

"At least we know about the quiz," Grace says, looping her arm through mine. We walk side by side down the hall, Tucker trailing behind us. "And you know what to expect for the cancer checkup."

"That's true," I say. Even though I never like getting poked and prodded, I always leave these yearly checks feeling so good because it's just another year in remission. "And we have that thing on Saturday," I say cheerfully.

We push open the doors, blinking in the sunlight as we make our way to Tucker's truck and my old red Corolla.

"What thing on Saturday?" He asks, and for the first time in the past hour, I finally look at him.

"Your thing on Saturday," I say, hoping my cheeks don't go pink like they do so often when I'm embarrassed. I feel warm all over. I wasn't planning to tell him I was going to his show this weekend. I wanted it to be a surprise.

His eyes go slightly wider. "You're coming?"

"You're coming?" Grace squeals at the same time, jumping up and down. I nod, my eyes not leaving his.

"But what about our deal?" he asks. His words are harsh, like an accusation, and all the air rushes from my lungs. This is why it should have been a surprise.

"Deal's off," I say quietly, looking down at my feet.

When Tucker first moved here, Grace constantly teased me about how much I liked people who could sing. Because I was so embarrassed, my fourteen-year-old self had made a deal with him. He wouldn't watch me dance, and I wouldn't hear him sing. It's been three years, and we've both kept our end of the deal, though I'm not entirely sure why he did.

Nathan arrives at the cars a moment later. "I am so in love," he says, tossing his backpack into the backseat of my (our) car before stepping out again to join us.

"Oh yeah?" Grace asks, disentangling herself from me to talk to Nathan. While I consider both Nathan and Grace my best friends, the two have a bond that I have never been able to understand. They act more like twins than Nathan and I do most of the time.

Nathan starts telling her about some cute thing Emmett did when Tucker steps between me and Nathan, blocking my view.

"Deal's off?" he asks, his eyes searching mine. I know he wants me to elaborate. I know he's searching for more. But I'm not ready to give him more.

"Deal's off," I say quietly. I hope I look calm, because my heart is beating erratically in my chest as he looks down at me.

Tucker sounds slightly strangled when he asks, "Why?"

I lift my shoulder as if to say it's not a big deal, even if we both know it means something has changed. "Just changed my mind." I hope it sounds like I don't care much, because I'm not ready to tell him why I changed my mind. The real reason is that I'm tired of missing out on his weekly shows that so many people rave about. I'm done with my audition, so maybe there can be an *us*. But I'm not ready to unpack that yet.

"Why?" he asks again, but before I can answer, Shawn calls my name. We both turn to see him running toward us. He's looking at me like he always does when he needs to use me to make Libby jealous. Usually, I don't mind, but today I do.

"Hey babe," he says. I wince. Tucker flinches, jerking a half step back away from me.

"Hi," I say, wishing Tucker wasn't standing there. Then I'd tell Shawn to lose it and text me later instead.

"Will you come to a party with me on Friday?" he asks with puppy dog eyes.

"Friday nights are our nights with Rosie," Grace says, and I give her what I hope is a thankful smile. If he wants to go to a party, it means Libby will be there, and all around, that sounds like a terrible time.

"I know, but I really need Rosie to be there with me." When I look at Shawn's dark eyes again, I know that I need to be there because Libby will definitely be there. "Plus, we're going to that thing on Saturday, so you guys can hang out then, instead."

"Fine," Grace says, turning back to Nathan as if that settles it.

But the thing is, I don't want to go. I always end up being the designated driver because I don't like drinking. Plus, I generally sit alone on the couch while he hangs out with all his friends and flirts with Libby. It's not exactly what I call a good time, but I know I can't say no with how he's looking at me right now. "Okay."

"Awesome! Thanks, babe." Shawn hugs me before running back to his surf buddies standing at the edge of the parking lot.

I look at Tucker, who's staring at the ground.

"Can we go?" Nathan suddenly asks. "I'm supposed to help Dad set up his exhibit tonight, but I need to change first."

"Yup," I say. "See you two later." I wave.

"See ya!" Grace grins at us, oblivious to the thick air that seems to be surrounding Tucker and me. I look at him once I'm in my car. He's still standing between our cars, watching me. I give him what I hope is a friendly wave and smile before pulling out of the parking lot and heading home, ignoring the gnawing guilt in my stomach the entire time.

Why did I say yes to Shawn?

journal entries from sophomore year

FEBRUARY *11*

Dear Journal,

Today was a fairly normal day (minus part of it... we'll get to that).

Now that we're in high school, we get to buy roses for people during the week of Valentine's Day, which get delivered on the holiday. It's kind of stupid, but I still might have bought a rose for Shawn.

I've had a sort of crush on him since elementary school, and then Grace dared me to buy him a flower, and she never dares me to do anything, so I did it. So that's kind of crazy.

They also have dumb things like we did in middle school. Today was Hug a Friend day. Like, okay, I guess we'll all just hug each other. But Shawn did give me a hug (and Grace and Libby) so I guess it isn't completely stupid.

We still ride the bus since we're all freshmen and can't drive yet. Me and Nathan usually ride the bus home with Tucker and Grace, who live just down the street from us.

So we're talking about the school day and how we hugged when Tucker shared that he hasn't hugged anyone yet.

Grace freaked out cause, like, it's Hug a Friend day, and apparently she's really into school spirit now?

We get off the bus, and he hugs me!!

It was super quick and over before I even realized it was happening. But... Tucker hugged me!

Then... a little later, we were texting... and I'm just gonna write out the convo cause I kind of want to remember it... It started around 7:30 pm, just as I was finishing up at the studio.

Tucker: Hey.

Me: Hi.

T: How are you?

Me: Good. You?

T: I'm good.

Me: That's good.

This is how a lot of our convos start... even though we text all the time. IDK why we don't just continue our old conversations. IDK why we say hi every time. Like, we already have a text thread... anyway.

T: So... tell me something random.

Me: Like what?

T: Anything.

Me: Ummm...

Me: I passed my math test today.

T: That's kind of lame. I mean, not that you passed, but that that's what you told me.

Me: You said to say something random. That's random. :)

T: True, true.

Me: You tell me something then, if mine was so boring.

T: ...

Me: What??

T: I have a secret.

Me: Okay, now you have to tell me.

T: I like you.

My heart was beating crazy fast. I wasn't expecting that, like, at all. Sure, we flirted sometimes, but nothing to make me think he would actually say that. And then I said this (can I just hide forever?)

Me: I like you too... I think...
T: You think? :(
Me: I mean... I do.
T: But??
Me: I sent Shawn a flower.
T: Oh.
Me: Yeah. But I do like you.
T: Cool. :)
Me: Yeah. :)

So. There's that.
Now I'm going to go to bed and figure out what all of this means in the morning.
Love, Rosie

June 3
Dear Journal,
I went on my very first date tonight. Not with Tucker.
I still like him. I still think he likes me. But... after our conversation (the one I wrote about last time), I told him that I couldn't date him or anything because of dance. I told him I thought it would be better if we stayed just friends for now.
He agreed, or at least he said he did... so now we're just friends. We sometimes flirt still, but he's my friend. He hangs out with us a

lot, me and Grace and Nathan, and he really does fit into our group. He and I eat lunch a lot together cause Grace is with her other friends and Nathan usually eats with some of the other drama kids. We sit at the end of the B-wing hallway, which is usually pretty empty. Tucker makes me laugh every single day. He's always showing me new songs that we listen to by sharing his headphones. They're always country, which I didn't think I liked before now... but I guess I kind of do.

Anyway.

I went on a date tonight.

It was fine for a first date (Grace thinks it was lame). There was a group of us (three couples, six people) and we ate dinner at some tiny little place I'd never even heard of. It wasn't terrible, but it wasn't great. Then we went and watched some Avengers movie at one of the guys' houses. I don't know which one it was, I honestly had no clue what was going on the entire time.

My date's name is Ryan. The whole time, one of the girls (who I don't know) kept saying how cute it was that his name is Ryan and my name is Rosie. I think she might have been jealous. I'm not sure.

But I went on a date.

Mom was thrilled.

Yes. You read that right. She was thrilled I went on a date with someone who isn't Tucker, even though I'm only 14, and she is always talking about how that's too young to be dating. She's also convinced that Tucker is gonna wreck my life because of reasons she won't share with me, but she's made it very, very clear that I'm not allowed to date boys—especially not him.

But she was really, really happy when Ryan picked me up tonight. I don't think we'll go out again, though, because I'm pretty sure he likes that girl who kept talking about our names since he watched her most of our date. So. Yup.

Are first dates always like this? Weird, awkward, and a little uncomfortable? Or just for me? Grace has been on dates with Leo before, but they always sound so fun...

I went on a date, but not with Tucker. I don't know why I keep writing that or why that matters. Okay.

For real going to bed now, before Mom peeks in and wants to talk about my date...

Love, Rosie

June 17

Dear Journal,

I've only heard bits and pieces about what happened between Tucker and his dad, but today, he told me more of the story.

I guess growing up, he was always going to big shows that his dad was doing whenever he went on tour. This was before he started school, so he got to go more often. He idolized his dad. I mean, if my dad was a famous singer, I'd probably think the world of him, too.

But then, when Tucker was 7, his dad left for a tour and never came back. His mom told him that it wasn't his fault (he had been very worried about that) and that his dad just needed to figure some stuff out.

By this point, he was already taking guitar lessons because he loved music.

As he got older, it got harder to live in Nashville because his dad was still there, too, even if he never actually saw him. He performed at some smaller gigs in the summer, and then he got the call about a record deal.

Until then, I don't think he had ever really voiced how much he wanted to follow in his dad's footsteps and make it big. He was young and really humble (okay, he still is and I'm also making this sound like this was like 5 years ago, but it was just a few months before he moved here).

So he went to the studio. He started sharing his songs with the producer, and then his dad walked in! The producer jumped up and talked to his dad about how happy he was to be able to snag up Tucker Bensen this young, and kept saying thanks to his dad.

That's when he stormed out, furious. But I guess word got around and that's how Murphy became his manager and got him out to LA, but then that record deal fell through.

He really wants to do this whole music thing on his own. Even if his dad is famous, not many people know that yet and he doesn't really want them to.

And I can kinda see now why he really doesn't like his dad. After so many years of just being gone, he decides to swoop in and help Tucker's music career take off, just because he can. What a jerk.

I hope Tucker does get his dreams. I hope he can get whatever he wants, without the help of his lame father.

Love, Rosie

5

I TRY NOT to twitch as the MRI machine clanks and moves above me. I close my eyes and try to focus on the music the tech picked out for me. When he asked what station I wanted to listen to, I told him to pick, because I always let them choose the music.

Sometimes they'll pick a Spotify station that I like, and other days I know they chose music they're a fan of. Today we're listening to country music, and I can't decide if it's what the tech guy thought I would like, or what he likes. Because with his hipster glasses and styled hair, he doesn't really seem like the country type.

One song ends, and the next song that starts makes me think of Tucker. I squeeze my eyes shut even tighter. I do not want to be thinking about him right now, but my mind doesn't listen to me. As the words of the song fill my head, all I can picture is the two of us, sitting on a blanket, and him kissing me on the Fourth of July.

My eyes fly open.

"Just a few more minutes," the tech says into the microphone. I don't respond, since I'm not supposed to move. Instead, I close my eyes again. I force myself to think of ballet shoes. I tune out the music and mentally go through the first three minutes of my audition routine until the whirling of the machine finally stops.

44

I follow the tech back to the room where my parents and Nathan are waiting. I'm glad that they were all able to come today. Dad's sketching something on his iPad and Mom is holding one of those gossip magazines that she pretends to hate but actually loves. My brother is on his phone and he is the only one who looks up when I enter.

"The doctor will be here in a few," the tech tells us, but we all know that we could be sitting here for another hour at least. The MRI was the last part of my actual testing. My arm is already bruising where the nurse, new I think, had to poke me three times to draw the blood they needed today.

"How was it?" Nathan asks, and for a second I think he's asking about my kiss with Tucker, because that's where my mind still is. I blink the memory away; it's been eight months, you'd think it wouldn't be so burned into my mind. You'd think I could think about something else.

"The MRI?" I ask. He nods, and Mom looks up at me as I shrug. "Fun as always."

"I know you hate those things," she says, then goes back to looking at her magazine. I'm grateful she's here, but it stings a little that she doesn't seem to want to be here. Finally, Dad looks up. I've always been a daddy's girl. He's been my biggest cheerleader in the dancing world, and when I was sick before, he spent every single day and night at the hospital. He even used my tiny bathroom shower so he didn't have to leave. We ate the not-too-terrible cafeteria food together when I could stomach it. He was always there for me, and today he feels like the one solid thing I'm holding onto.

"It'll be fine, Rosebud," he says quietly, his blue eyes peering into mine. My heart rate slows a tad with the nickname that's always been just his.

I nod, though I don't quite believe him, even if his words somewhat calm me. We go through this routine every year. He's calm and steady, while Mom reads the latest celebrity gossip they always leave in the rooms—pretending not to be anxious while we all know she actually is—and Nathan moves his leg up and down, no hiding how he's feeling.

I'm a ball of nerves, too, as I twist my hands in my lap and we wait for Doctor Barker to come in with the preliminary results.

Finally, the door opens, she says hello to all of us, asks Dad how painting is going and Mom about ballet. She asks about my audition and then she sits down on the rolling stool that I used to love playing on as a kid.

"Okay," she says, after Nathan cracks a joke about how school is going. We all go still, just like every year. I've been holding my breath and I know I won't let it out until she says I'm clear.

But the words don't come. Not those ones anyway.

There's a faint buzzing noise that seems to fill the room right after she says, "I'm so sorry, Rosie, but you've got one tumor..." Then all I can hear is the buzzing. I see her lips moving, and Dad's face go white, but I can't hear anything else.

All I can think is *the cancer is back, the cancer is back, the cancer is back.* And I am not okay.

I'm quiet on the way home. Nathan holds my hand as we take the freeway back down to San Clemente. Doctor Barker promised that she'd call about my treatment plan on Monday.

I'm going to die, I think, even though I know that's not what Doctor Barker said. She said it is common for cancer to show up again. It doesn't always happen, but it isn't surprising when it does. She promised I'll get the best care and treatment and that first they'll remove the tumor to see if any other treatment is even necessary—like possible radiation—since that's the only thing that came back on the scans and bloodwork, and Dad promised we'll fight this together.

My phone vibrates in my lap; Nathan reaches for it and types in my passcode. I'm not even mad because my whole body seems to be frozen.

"Grace and Tucker want to know how it went." Suddenly, energy zaps back into me and I grab my phone from his hands.

The Four Musketeers Group Chat

GRACE

Any word?

TUCKER

Rosie???

All clear. :)

I send the text and turn my phone over, ignoring the concern on Nathan's face.

"Why did you do that?" he asks, and Mom turns to look at us. "She just lied and told them everything is fine." Nathan is mad, and Dad glances back at me for a split second.

I swallow hard. "I'm still processing." Which is true. "I will tell them, but not over text. Not today."

"You need to tell them," he says gently, but I can feel his anger beneath the words.

"I will," I promise. I hope the words don't sound as empty as I feel, because I have no intention of telling them yet. Maybe I won't even have to, maybe after the surgery, I'll get the real all clear, and I'll be completely fine and won't have to share anything.

"Okay," he says, and I know he doesn't believe me.

"Just don't say anything yet, any of you," I say and everyone nods in promise. If they don't agree, no one says so.

6

MY HANDS ARE SHAKING with anger. I clench them into fists to stop the movement. It's well after midnight, but I pull up Tucker's info in my phone and call him. He answers after two rings.

"Can you come get me?" I ask, moving away from the loud speaker in the kitchen. I head to the back patio and into the cool winter air, but there are people everywhere. I just want to go home. I want to be alone and not at this stupid party.

"Yeah," he answers, without missing a beat. "Text me the address."

"I'm in Newport," I say quietly. Shame washes through me, and I'm embarrassed that I got myself stuck up here, even though it's mostly not my fault.

"I'll be there soon," he says, and I share my location with him. Walking back inside, I avoid three different couples who are making out in the front room and go sit on the front porch to wait for him, even though he probably won't be here for another hour.

I hug my knees to my chest, grateful I decided to bring a jacket, even though Shawn laughed when he saw it. I groan. It's nights like tonight that make me, and everyone around me, question why I'm even trying to date him. Why did I let Mom pressure me into this? When will I stop letting her control every aspect of my life, including who I should or shouldn't date?

"I have freaking cancer," I whisper into the night and wrap my arms tighter around myself. I will not cry, not right now, not tonight. I haven't cried yet and this party was supposed to be a distraction from the news I got earlier. It was supposed to be fun; at least, Shawn promised it would be fun. And Mom said that I could go, because it was with Shawn. But I'm learning more and more that parties and me don't mix. I really need to stop coming with him. I really need to stop letting us use each other for our own selfish gain. It's not worth it anymore.

My phone vibrates; the notification is from Shawn on Snapchat, so I turn my phone over. It'll be a pitch-black picture that's supposed to be him and his drunk friends. I want to turn my phone off, but I don't in case Tucker calls. Instead, I put it in my pocket and try to think about anything besides the fact that my cancer is back. But my mind keeps going back to it. I know that the surgery will make my body weaker, at least for a few weeks, but I don't know what a tumor means going forward. Will I need more tests? Will there be more tumors? Will I have to do chemo again? My chin hits my chest in defeat and I listen to the beat of the music blasting behind me.

I've got my face buried in my hands when I hear the familiar hum of Tucker's truck. I'm down the front pathway and at the street as he pulls up, and I climb in.

"Hey," he says, and I look up and briefly meet his eyes, which are full of questions.

I glance away. "Thanks for picking me up, Tuck."

"Of course," he says as we pull out of the neighborhood, passing houses that could swallow three of mine. Now that he's here, I might actually cry. Tonight didn't go like it was supposed to. We're pulling onto the nearly empty highway when I let out a sigh.

"Wanna tell me what happened?" I feel his eyes on me for a split second.

I sigh again. "Not really, but since it's nearly one in the morning and you just drove half an hour to get me, I guess I should." I pause, not knowing what to say exactly. "Shawn has a friend up in Newport who told us about the party. I wanted to stay home. I didn't do super great on the math quiz and I was really tired from the hospital." I pause. "But Mom told me I should go; practically pushed me out the door."

He grunts. It's always been apparent that my mom is willing to let me hang out with other guys on our own, just not with him. Which bothers him. And me, if I'm honest about it.

"And your tests went alright?" he asks, avoiding the hypocrisy of my mother.

I force myself to smile, thankful it's dark, so he probably won't see it. "All clear. But Shawn really wanted to come to the party."

"So you went." I can't tell what he's feeling—annoyed, maybe? He's white-knuckling the steering wheel.

"So I went. Shawn drove me, Russ, and Libby. Russ and Libby took off to mingle as soon as we got to the party. Shawn handed me a warm beer and then left me to find his friends."

"Does he not know that you don't drink?" he asks me, reminding me that Shawn doesn't know much about me, and he doesn't even care.

I shake my head. "No, I think he knows but sometimes forgets, and then he always says that I need to at least hold a cup, or else people will think I'm not 'cool.'" I hold up my hands and put the words in quotes.

He opens his mouth, probably to tell me how many things are wrong with that sentence, but I keep talking.

"About an hour later I was still sitting on the couch by myself, music blasting through the house and couples making out and drinking. About ten minutes before I called you, I got up to find Shawn to see when we would be leaving." Anger slips into my voice. "I found him in the kitchen with a bunch of guys he called his buddies, but I'd never seen them before. He was completely wasted. Which made me mad, since he said he'd be designated driver and he hates it when anyone else drives his car.

"He sees me and says, 'Hey, Rosiebaby.' His words were slurring together." I shudder—I can't help it. "It's not a great nickname to begin with. I asked how we're gonna get home, and he says, 'We're not going home, we're going surfing.'"

"It's the middle of the night," he interjects.

"Obviously," I say, shaking my head. "He's an idiot, they're all idiots. Then, as he was following his new buddies out the door, he yelled that I should probably find another ride home. So I called you."

"So you called me," Tucker says. Part of me really wants him to ask *why*, even though I'm not sure I want to tell him.

"Thanks for coming. I know I said that already, but thank you. Mom would have killed me if she knew I was stuck up in Newport at one in the morning."

"Where does she think you are?"

"Hanging out with Shawn, but in town, not all the way up here. But anyway, thanks for coming. I knew you'd figure that Shawn was involved and I know you don't like him."

His fingers turn white again as he grips the steering wheel. "Why are you with him?" he whispers a few moments later.

"I'm not, not really," I whisper back, tugging on my fingers. Seconds ago, I wanted him to ask me this, why I'm trying to date Shawn, and why I called him to pick me up. But suddenly I'm too tired to have this conversation. I can't add this conversation to the list of things that happened today.

"Help me understand then." He nearly pleads. "I thought this year would be our year. You and me. Did all that stuff we said before Paris not matter? Did our kiss mean nothing to you? Instead you're trying to date that jack—jerk?"

I'm stunned for a minute—what am I supposed to say to that?

That I thought it would be our year, too, that I hoped it could be, but that after our kiss my mom got after me about dating him? "You know it meant something to me, Tucker," I finally say.

"Do I, though?" The words slice through me. "Then why do you want him to be your boyfriend and not me? You know how I feel about you, and up until Paris, I thought you felt the same."

"I did." I'm watching him now, and as we pass under a street light, I see that he is pale. "I do. But it's better this way." Why am I trying to convince both of us of that? While I was waiting for him to come pick me up, I was thinking about being brave and not letting Mom control my life.

I have cancer now though, I remind myself, *so it* is *better this way.*

He chokes. "Better for who? Your mom? You can't let her control everything about your life, Rosie."

He's right. I know he's right, but admitting that will change everything between us. And what if things go badly and then he and I aren't even friends anymore?

I can't come up with anything else to say, so we're silent the rest of the way home.

Dad is waiting up when I get back to the house. "You have a good time with Shawn?" he asks.

"Yup," I say stiffly, as we hear Tucker's truck pulling out of the driveway. "It was great."

He doesn't ask me why Tucker brought me home, and I'm thankful for that. I head upstairs and lie down on my bed, fully clothed, and that's when the tears finally start to flow.

7

IT'S Dad's idea to go out for lunch.

I spent the morning sleeping, thanks to my late night, and we haven't talked about yesterday at all. It feels weird though, to be out in public like this. Yet also not weird, because it's just so *us*. Dad copes with hard things by eating good food, and since my parents don't love cooking, eating out is just kind of what we do. Even when things are weird and sad and we have to talk about the tumor that's growing by my liver.

We're sitting at South of Nick's, waiting for our entrees when Nathan finally breaks the silence.

"Remember that time we drove up the coast because Rosie didn't believe the ocean was that big?" Nathan asks, smiling at the memory.

I would smile, too, if it didn't make me think about having cancer the first time around.

"Yes," Dad says, before I can shut down this particular conversation. "And then you both cried when we said it was time to turn around and drive back home."

Nathan laughs. "I only cried because I liked being in the car; it meant I could watch movies on that little portable DVD player we had."

I see Mom's eyes light up. "I'd forgotten about that thing. I was so busy that trip, trying to come up with the routines for our next show at the studio."

"You were pretty cranky," Nathan says.

"I was not," Mom argues.

Dad chuckles. "You were kind of cranky. Then on the way home, Rosie threw up all over."

I bury my face in my hands. "That was not my proudest moment." I want to say that I threw up because I was so nervous about having cancer, that even though I was only seven, I knew it was something big and scary. But I don't want to talk about being sick right now, especially when I feel fine. I want to keep on pretending that it doesn't exist—if only my brain would get the memo.

Everyone laughs and our food arrives, so we don't have to talk about how I'm sick again, or my possible treatment plans, or my future with dance. My stomach flips as I stare at my veggie enchilada.

I hadn't thought about what this means for dance yet. It's taken every moment since I was in remission to get to where I am now. Surgery plus recovery time will not make my body stronger. I'm going to have to work even harder when I get to Paris—if I get in—just to be at the level I'm at now.

"You okay, Rosie?" My brother jostles my arm with his elbow.

"What? Fine," I say and pick up my knife and fork, taking a bite just to prove it. But inside, I'm not doing fine. So much for pretending I'm not sick.

Dad reaches across the table and gently squeezes my hand. "It's okay to not be fine, Rosebud." And just like yesterday, when everything went fuzzy after I heard the news, the clatters from the kitchen and the chatter around us fade away and it's like we're the only people here.

"I'm scared," I admit, and immediately Nathan has an arm around my shoulder.

"You should have stayed home last night," Mom says stiffly, but she won't look at me, and that's when I realize that even with all of her makeup, her eyes are puffy. She must have spent most of the night crying. I want to call her out, since she was the one who told me to go out last night with Shawn. She told me several times that it was "a great idea."

Instead, I look down at the table. "I don't want to think about what Doctor Barker said. I can't think about what she said. I feel fine." Which is true, because the last time I was sick, we knew something was wrong because I felt tired and sore all the time, and, well—sick.

Right now though, I feel fine. Physically, anyway. A little more tired than normal, but I've also been dancing a lot more than usual.

"Maybe you just think you feel fine," Mom says.

"I feel fine," I snap, because I need her to believe me. "Maybe I do have a tumor, but all I know is that right now I feel healthy and fine and on top of the world because I know I'm going to get into the Paris Academy." I swallow back a sob. "But we don't know what's gonna happen with my cancer and it's all kind of shitty."

"*Rosie*," Mom cries. She hates when we swear and the couple at the table next to us glances our way. But this whole situation isn't exactly sunshine and roses, and while I want to pretend that I'm not sick, maybe facing reality would be better.

"What? It's true that I feel fine. True that my chances of getting into Paris are high. I don't want to have cancer because that will only set my career back."

Everyone is quiet for a moment.

"You have to do whatever Doctor Barker says," Nathan says, so quietly that Dad leans forward to hear better. "So that you will be okay."

I give a jerky nod. "Okay, then what? What if it's more than just a tumor? Then all of my training the last nine years will be for what? Nothing? I might not be strong enough to dance in the fall even if the cancer goes away completely. Paris is over." The tears fall then and I know I'm not crying about the cancer or the possibility of it being worse than we know right now. I'm crying because my one and only dream is being taken from me, and there's absolutely nothing I can do about it.

"It's not over," Nathan says, his voice calm and soothing. "We'll help get you back to where you are, even if it takes a little longer to get to Paris."

I nod, even though I know that if they find out I'm sick, they'll fill my spot, and if they don't take me this year, I'll be too old to join the program.

Mom knows this, too, but thankfully, she stays silent.

"Let's just wait and see what Doctor Barker says. She mentioned that surgery would be the best option, and maybe the only thing you have to do since there was no evidence of cancer anywhere else," Dad says finally. "Let's not worry about ballet until we know more. And, who knows—maybe they've made a lot of great strides in the past eight years." Dad smiles, optimistic. "So even if it's more than a tumor, it'll be faster and easier to kick cancer's butt."

But I know that now he's just lying to himself. He may be the artist of the family, but he reads nearly every article that comes out about treating the cancer I had as a kid, even if I have been in remission for nine years. He knows that while they're learning new things, there still isn't a guaranteed cure.

"Maybe," I say finally, because I'm still crying and I can't stand to break his heart, too. That would be too much, and it all feels like too much, and even though there's the nagging part in my brain telling me that I'm making it worse than it actually is, it still feels bad.

I eat what I can of my lunch, and Nathan's arm stays around my shoulders the whole time. Mom avoids eye contact with all of us, and Dad smiles and talks about his favorite memories and tells us about his next art show. There are a few brief moments where everything feels like a normal Saturday afternoon, but they are fleeting because my brain won't shut up.

I have cancer. I have cancer. I have cancer. I have cancer. I have cancer.

8

DAD'S READING the newspaper in his oversized chair when I get to the bottom of the stairs. I'm wearing my favorite floral dress and denim jacket that Nathan found at a yard sale two years ago.

"Hey, Rosebud." Dad gives me a cheery smile that brings a lump to my throat. No matter what happens in the next few months, I know he's going to handle it all with a smile. That's just how he is.

"Hey, Daddy," I say, feeling like a little girl again. I give him a quick hug before I plop on the couch next to him. Nathan is still upstairs getting ready and I'd rather sit and wait than stand in the hallway and wait.

"You going to tell them tonight?" he asks, watching me intently. My heart stops for a second; how can he know that I want to tell Tucker my feelings for real? Then it hits me—he's asking about the tumor, not my crush. He said *them,* as in Grace and Tucker, not just *him.* I shake my head.

"No, not yet." I run my hands over my legs, one of my anxious habits. I'm not ready to have a conversation with them about the tumor. "I just don't know how to tell them. It doesn't feel real yet. I think I'm still adjusting to the news, ya know?"

He nods. "I am too."

I think of lunch, how the mood felt so somber as we left because there are still so many unanswered questions.

"I *will* tell them soon," I promise, only because I know I do need to tell them. Even if it is only this tumor. They are my best friends. They deserve to know, but I'm not ready. "I just need to let it sit more."

"Maybe after next week, once we have a plan, it'll be easier." He gives me a smile that makes me feel like I've made him proud and disappointed him at the same time.

"Maybe," I say, then stand as Nathan comes running down the stairs.

I grab my purse but Dad stops me with his hand on mine. "I love you, Rosie," he says and I blink rapidly so the tears that fill my eyes won't fall.

"I love you, too, Dad," I say and he smiles at me.

"You two have fun," he says. All I can muster is a nod in reply before following Nathan outside.

I smooth out my dress and look around the bar for Grace. Nathan sees her first and I follow him to a booth near the small stage. Several people say hello to him as we walk by, since a lot of our classmates are here. Once a week, the local bar hosts an alcohol-free happy hour for the high school students. It's one of the nights where Tucker sings as their main entertainment. A lot of people talk about it at school, and Grace and Nathan come almost every week. But tonight's my first time.

Shawn said he'd be here, but after last night, I made it clear that I'll be sitting with my friends, if I can help it.

"She lives!" Grace jumps up to hug me when I reach the table.

"Only joking, but I'm glad you took a break from ballet and Shawn for the evening."

I hug her back. "You know I've missed hanging out with you on Saturdays."

She releases me, and pulls my twin in for a hug. Over his shoulder she says, "I know, me too." As she releases him and slides back into the booth, she tilts her head in a gesture I know all too well. It means 'you should stop hanging out with Shawn and you'd get your Saturdays back.'

I nod, because she's right. I want to tell her it's my mom who wants me to date Shawn, and that I'm done with that. I want to date someone else. Tucker. I glance around the bar for him, but he's nowhere to be found in the sea of people.

"Where's Tucker?" I ask and Grace raises an eyebrow at me. I want to tell *him* first about how I'm feeling, not Grace. But the words bubble up in my chest. I open my mouth again when a soft hand touches my shoulder.

"Right here," he says. I turn in surprise. He looks good; he's in a white T-shirt and is wearing a cowboy hat. I suppress a shiver and keep my eyes on his face after my quick once-over.

"Glad you could all make it." His words are light, but his eyes don't leave mine. He leans in close and I get a whiff of his minty gum and woodsy cologne. His breath tickles my ear as he whispers, "You look pretty, darlin'. But what I really want to know is when can I see you dance?" His voice is cold and unforgiving, like he's mad at me even though the question seems innocent. Even though he said I'm pretty. He's mad I'm breaking the deal that I made.

He takes half a step back, eyeing me.

"Whenever you want," I mumble, glancing down at my feet. Because I can't talk to him about this, not now. Yes, I'm breaking the deal. I think he only agreed in the first place because he was worried I'd completely walk away from a friendship with him if he said no, and I honestly might have. I knew from the first second I laid my eyes on Tucker Bensen that he was someone special—that he was going to be someone special to me. But now, the deal is off. I'm here and I'm going to hear him sing. We can work out the details of him watching me dance later.

"Are you practicing tomorrow?" he asks and I look back up at him. Someone calls his name, but he holds up a finger.

I let out a sigh. "No, I'm not. We're all just hanging out at home—" I start, but Grace interrupts.

"Oh, as a celebration for everything being clear yesterday?" Her grin cracks my heart in two.

"Something like that." I glance at my feet again, and my cheeks grow warm. Now would be the perfect time to tell them. Instead, I say, "But I'll be in the studio every day next week, and you're welcome to come by any time."

"I think I will." Tucker knocks on the table before walking toward the stage where a woman, possibly his boss, stands watching us.

I sink onto the bench across from Grace and Nathan.

Both have their eyes on me. "Okay, what's with the ice storm?" Grace asks.

"Nothing," I say. "I mean, I don't know."

"Liar."

I let out a sigh. "Tucker had to pick me up last night."

Her mouth pops into the perfect O. "Shawn is an idiot," she mutters, rolling her eyes. Again, I'm reminded of how my friends, but especially Grace, don't understand why I've been 'trying' to date Shawn. I want to tell her the truth, that it is all a sham and that I'm officially ending it, tonight. I'm also worried about telling her the truth about my cancer, and that I'm nervous to risk changing things with Tucker. What if it all goes wrong? It could go so horribly wrong. I close my eyes, trying to keep my mind from spiraling any more than it already is.

I make up my mind. Tonight, I'm going to tell Shawn he can do whatever the heck he wants, despite what our moms say and in spite of his crush on Libby, and then I'm going to tell Tucker how

I feel. I'm going to take the jump. I have too many secrets; I have to let at least one of them out.

"Shawn went surfing at midnight," I say, only confirming what she just said about him being an idiot. She rolls her eyes a second time.

"You should dump him or end whatever this is with him. I can't ever keep it straight if you're actually with him or not," she says and I blink in surprise. "He's no good for you, and like... you haven't held hands with him for weeks. When was the last time you even kissed? *Have* you even kissed?"

Nathan is watching me intently now, too, waiting for the answer. He knows the truth, but he's my twin, so of course he hasn't told her that it's mostly just a sham. She may be his best friend, but we're even closer than that because we shared a womb.

Never, I think, because that was one of our rules: no kissing. "We kiss in private," I say to them, but I feel my cheeks turn red from the lie. Nathan raises his eyebrows. I wish that we actually had twin telepathy so I could tell him that I've never kissed Shawn. The only guy I've ever kissed is Tucker.

"I never knew you were such a private person about affection." Grace mistakes my red cheeks for embarrassment. "I'm your best friend and even when you two hang out with us, you don't hold hands; you don't even flirt. You and Tucker have more chemistry than you and Shawn ever have, and you two are just friends."

My cheeks have got to be bright red now with how much they're burning. I glance down. Why does this feel so bad to hear her talk about me and Shawn like this? I wonder if Mom even believes that I like him, if my best friend can't even see the feelings I've been trying to pretend to have. I look at the clock hanging above the bar, wondering when the show will start, and trying to figure out how to stall and not answer her accusation.

I don't know how to tell her that I think I'm in love with her cousin. I don't know how to tell Tucker that I want to be with him, but *oh hey, also my cancer is back, so you know, I'm the sick girl again.*

I can't tell her, or anyone, about my deal with Shawn and our moms, since it's been going on for five months now—longer than either of us expected, but he's more than happy to have someone on his arm that makes Libby jealous. Grace would tell me that we're just using each other, that we should be honest, and that we're kind of pathetic. Grace lives in a world where fairy tales have happy endings, but that's not how real life works. I live in a world where my cancer is back after nine years of remission. And even if I wasn't sick, I'd be going to Paris in August and Tucker will be in the States, most likely touring or at least opening for someone else.

I have cancer. I have cancer. I have cancer. I have cancer.

The words match my heartbeat and break up any thoughts I was having about Tucker. I look at Nathan, knowing he'll be able to read my mind. But I've been quiet for too long.

Nathan fidgets. I force myself to keep my hands still. Grace notices. "What's going on with you two?" She glances at me first and then to Nathan, who's staring at me. I give the slightest shake of my head. I am *not* about to tell her here.

"I broke up with Emmett," Nathan says and I try to keep my mouth from dropping open. I have to pretend like I know this news. I should know this news. Breaking up with his first boyfriend is a big deal, and I thought he was happy.

"What? *Why?*" She nearly shouts as she punches Nathan in the shoulder. People at the neighboring table glance at us before returning to their conversation. "Did he do something? If he did something, I'm gonna kick his butt." Grace raises a fist and looks around the bar which makes Nathan smile; she wouldn't be able to hurt a fly even if she wanted to. But she'd still give it a try if it meant protecting someone she loved.

"I just don't think we're a good fit." Nathan focuses on the sugar packet in his hand, moving it along the table.

"But you were so in love with him yesterday," she says. "What happened?"

He gives a limp smile and glances at me. He broke up with his boyfriend because of *me*. Because I have a tumor and he doesn't know what the future holds. I swallow a lump in my throat.

"I just feel like I might need some time to figure stuff out," he says, still looking at me. I squirm. I don't want him to break up with his boyfriend because he's stressed about me. I know that he'll be anxious and worried about me being sick and then he'll be anxious that his anxiety is ruining his relationship. This is his way of shutting things down before Emmett has a chance to walk away, proving Nathan's biggest fear correct—that having anxiety somehow makes him unlovable.

"How come you didn't tell me last night? I knew something was off, but I didn't want to ask," she says before I can jump in.

"Just wasn't ready to talk about it," he answers, his green eyes never leaving mine. "Sometimes talking about the hard stuff is hard, but it also feels good. I already feel better knowing you two know about it."

Grace is oblivious to the silent conversation that Nathan is having with me.

"We'll always be here for you," she says and gives him a side hug, but he still holds my gaze. I want to pull away, but I can't seem to. Grace continues to babble, unaware of what my brother is trying to tell me. "I think you should still give him a chance, but that's totally up to you."

I'm the first to look away. I'm not ready to say anything—not yet, not here, not tonight. It's a conversation that needs to happen in private, not public.

I sink into my seat as the woman onstage with Tucker takes the microphone and announces him. I swallow my feelings, the news about my tumor, and just *everything*. I don't want to think about any of it right now. I'm here to watch Tucker perform for the very first time.

9

MY HEART THUMPS wildly as Tucker takes the stage, pulling the stool away from the microphone as he gets settled. He looks like a real country singer up on the stage and I imagine where he'll be a few years from now. Filling up stadiums, probably.

"There she is." I jump in my seat at the sound of Shawn's voice. Tonight I want to stay with my friends and enjoy watching Tucker perform, but the look on Shawn's face tells me that won't be an option.

"Stand in the front with me, babe?" he asks.

I nod with slight defeat, too tired to argue with him, and slide across the booth seat, giving what I hope is an apologetic look to Grace and Nathan who look both sad and disappointed that I'm going with Shawn again. Maybe this will be my chance to talk to him though, to tell him that I'm done with our little charade and done with my mom dictating who I can or can't like and date.

As we approach the group of people standing in front of the stage, Tucker catches my eye and winks as he pulls the microphone toward him. I look up to see if Shawn noticed, but he's already talking to Russ about going surfing later. Apparently surfing at midnight is fun (and incredibly stupid) and thrilling (and incredibly stupid) and Shawn has to do it again (because he's an idiot). I roll my eyes, grateful he's at least not trying to hold my hand.

"Howdy, y'all," Tucker says into the mic and nearly everyone cheers. He's added a bit more twang into his voice. You wouldn't think that most of my classmates have a thing for country music, but I think there's something they like about being here when he performs. Plus, he's nothing like his father, so I think that helps a bit. He's one of us, but he's not, because he's already got an agent and a possible record deal. Everyone sort of idolizes him; they want to be him even though not many people actually know him. He likes to write and sing. He wants to share his music with the world, but he doesn't want to be in the spotlight every second of the day.

My stomach flutters nervously. Tonight, in just a few seconds, I get to hear him sing live for the first time in my life. Yes, I broke our deal one year ago when I watched his one and only YouTube video, a cover of a song I didn't know, so technically, I have heard him sing. But not even Nathan knows I watched it. I'll take that secret to my grave. I think Tucker would hate me if he knew I broke the deal I was so adamant about making. But tonight will be the first time I hear him sing live.

"I'm happy to be here with y'all tonight." As he speaks, I can picture him in a stadium that's packed with people. "I've got a nice set planned for you tonight, so let's get started." He's not going to be singing in random bars during their non-alcoholic happy hour forever. He strums his guitar and opens his mouth. His voice is like warm butter. He's not meant for small things; as he reaches the chorus, I know that he's going to make it big.

He must know this, too, I think, with how hard he's worked to get an agent. But he never brags about it; he just says he's grateful that he's lucky enough to do what he loves.

It makes me wish I was a little humbler about dance; I'm kind of a snob about how good I am. But hey, I know that I shouldn't be so cocky about it, so that counts for something, right?

I lose myself to Tucker's voice. He mostly sings covers, which

Grace says is normal. She told me that occasionally he'll share an original, but those he keeps pretty close to his heart, waiting for the record deal to come.

I close my eyes and let my head fall back as he sings—his singing voice is just a deeper and richer version of his normal voice, and it gives me goosebumps. When I open my eyes again, I realize that Shawn is gone, and for the moment, I don't care. Tucker looks down at me several times throughout the night, sending a thrill through my body each time his eyes meet mine. Each time he gives me a soft smile—one that's reserved just for me.

I always said I didn't like country music, but hearing Tucker sing makes me wonder if I was wrong.

His set is nearly over when Shawn appears beside me again, and one look at his swollen lips tells me everything I need to know. I look around and see Libby standing by her friends, her hair slightly mussed. I let out a huff of frustration.

"Having fun?" I ask sarcastically. Couldn't he at least make a better effort to pretend to like me so that our parents are happy? Our parents might not be here, but still.

Shawn just grins and takes my hand as Tucker leans into the mic to talk. "This last song is for one of my best friends." He looks at me and says, "This one's for you, Rosie."

I pull my hand from Shawn's grasp.

One of Shawn's friends yells, "He's trying to steal your girl, man." Even though he probably knows exactly what Shawn was just doing with Libby. It's no secret how Tucker feels about me, it's no secret the chemistry we've always shared. Shawn just laughs and I know my face is bright red from embarrassment, anger, and a tiny bit of humiliation.

Tucker starts to play and it's not a song I recognize, but once he starts singing, it's pretty clear by the lyrics that this song isn't meant to woo me. The song is all about what love ain't, and I know Tucker's telling me that what I've got isn't love, even if I already know that. He doesn't know that I know that. He doesn't know that the way I feel about *him* doesn't even hold a candle to the non-existent feelings I have for Shawn.

"Wanna tell me what's going on with you two?" Shawn asks when the song is over, his breath hot in my ear. I suppress a shiver of annoyance.

"He likes me," I say honestly, and as Shawn looks a little miffed, it occurs to me that maybe part of this situation isn't completely fake for him, even if he was just making out with Libby. Maybe there's a thrill there that comes from her not actually being his. Of sort of being with someone else. He's the type of guy who wants to have as many girls fawning over him as possible.

Realization of something covers Shawn's face. "He's in love with you," he says. Tucker waves to the crowd and heads off the stage. "You should be with him."

"Are you fake dumping me?" I hiss at Shawn, surprised. The noise of the crowd starts to fade as I zone in on him. This is what I was supposed to do, he wasn't supposed to beat me to it.

He's right." Shawn looks down at me with a sad sort of smile. "What we have isn't love, it's not even real, and it's never going to be real." He walks away without another word, toward Libby and his other friends.

For a few seconds, I remain frozen and stunned. I should feel crushed; that's what you're supposed to feel when you get dumped, even if it wasn't technically a relationship. But instead I feel the blush on my cheeks spread to the rest of my face, which could be mistaken for a tomato right now. Everyone near me seems to be staring straight at me, wondering what I'm going to do. I don't even know why I feel embarrassed right now— maybe because of the song Tucker just sang that called me out on my crap? Or the fact that while I wanted to end things with Shawn, I had no clue he was thinking about doing the same.

Do I go after the boy who just sang me a song or head after the boy I've supposedly been sort of dating for the past five months?

I turn and head down the small hallway that leads to the backstage area where Tucker headed. I find him standing in the middle of a small room. His back is to me as he sets his guitar in its case.

"What was that exactly?" My voice comes out an octave higher and louder than I intend, startling him. He turns, and I can't read his expression.

"The truth."

I look down at the faded pink carpet, too embarrassed to meet his eyes right now.

"Can't you feel what happens between us, whenever we're together?" he asks quietly, taking a step toward me. His faded black boots knock against the toes of my sneakers, but I can't look up at him. "It can't be the same with him. I can tell that it's not the same with him."

I don't say anything, because of course he's right, but I'm feeling too many things right now. I swallow, closing my eyes. *Be brave,* I think.

"I'm sorry if I embarrassed you," he says, his hand coming under my jaw and tilting my face to look at him. "That wasn't my intention."

"I–I'm not embarrassed just because of you," I stammer. Instead, I say, "I caught him making out with Libby right before you sang that song."

His gaze shifts from something I don't know how to interpret into anger. "I'm gonna kill him."

I hold back a smile. "Then you sang that song and he broke up with me." The words hang heavy in the air. Can I even call it a breakup if we weren't actually together? Calling it anything less, though, makes me feel dumb for going along with the charade in the first place.

"He what?" Tucker's eyes go wide.

"I don't want to date him," I say quietly. "I'm single, but my heart belongs to someone else."

His eyes flare.

"Single?" he asks, as if he's testing the word, making sure it feels right on his tongue. Guess he's gonna ignore the part where I said my heart belongs to someone else— that my heart belongs to him.

"Single," I repeat.

"It's about damn time," he says, searching my face, and he must find whatever he's looking for, because he takes a step closer. My breath hitches as he closes the distance between us and his gaze flicks to my lips. I lick them in anticipation.

My pulse races. For a split second I'm afraid that someone is going to come through the door and stop whatever is about to happen, but no one does, and a moment later, his lips are on mine.

He tastes like the spearmint gum that he's always chewing, and I smile against his lips. I feel him smile in return, before he pulls me closer, deepening the kiss, and my lips part slightly as he runs his tongue across my lips and I shiver; but he doesn't deepen the kiss any more than that.

I'm standing on my toes, my hands in his hair, tightening around the soft curls that hit the base of his neck and pulling him closer. He has his arms firmly around my back, pulling me against him.

Warmth spreads through my body as he kisses me, and for a moment, I don't think about Shawn or cancer or being embarrassed. He shifts, lifting me a few inches off the ground before he pulls away slightly, our foreheads touching. "I've been wanting to do that for so long," he whispers.

Instead of replying, I lean forward and kiss him again. Because for the moment, the only thing that matters is kissing Tucker Bensen.

10

NATHAN HOLDS my hand as we silently ride to the hospital for my first group therapy session after school. Doctor Barker recommended I go, as a second-time cancer patient, because she thinks it will help me come to terms with what is happening in my body. Which, to be completely honest, is fair, since I'm still deep in denial that I even have a tumor. Mostly, I just pretend it isn't there.

I'm also still not sure how I'll hide my surgery and recovery from Tucker and Grace, but I'll be damned if they find out sooner than I want them to. Plus, I still have another week till the surgery, and once it's all over, I can tell them about it. It's not that much time.

Thinking about Tucker makes my palms sweat, but in a good way, I think. After we kissed on Saturday, I ran away and we haven't talked since beyond a handful of heart emojis. I haven't told anyone yet. I want to tell my brother, but I don't really know how to say it. Shawn ended our fake sort of almost relationship and then I went and let Tucker kiss me immediately after that?

I know Nathan and Grace won't judge me in any way, but I'm not ready for the "oh you two are perfect together" that I know we'll get from Grace. I just want to enjoy this for as long as I can. I just want to be us—Rosie and Tucker—without anyone else knowing about whatever we are. Without having to tell him the truth about what's happening to my body, and maybe for just a few days, that kiss can be just ours.

Dad walks into the clinic with me, while Nathan stays in the car. Mom didn't come; she had classes at the studio. Dad will have to sit in the waiting area or hang out in the car with Nathan, but he stays with me until they are ready to take me back.

"You'll do great, kid," he whispers in my ear as he gives me a hug.

I follow the nurse to a large room full of chairs in a semicircle. There's one girl my age sitting right in the middle and she grins at me as I walk in.

I swallow hard; today is not a day for tears. Today I can be brave, plus Doctor Barker said I didn't have to talk if I didn't want to, so hopefully I can just listen today. But being here feels like I'm embracing this reality, that I do have another tumor, and my last appointment wasn't just a bad dream.

I walk toward the girl, pausing for a half-second when I realize she's in a hospital gown. They didn't give me one, but do I need one?

She catches my pause and smiles. "It's okay, I'll probably be the only one in a gown." She's got a bubbly voice that could rival Grace's.

"Oh," is all I say as I take the seat next to her before I can change my mind.

"I'm Lucy," she says. "I'm here full time right now. In the hospital, I mean. I'm doing chemo but my mom doesn't really have the capacity to help me when I'm at home. She's got the money though, so I just stay here."

I shift nervously. "I'm sorry," I say, but that doesn't feel like the right thing to say. I'm just not sure how to respond.

Lucy smiles again. "It's alright. I've got a brain tumor that keeps getting bigger right on my brain stem, plus one that's growing by my lung, but they're gonna take that out this week. You?"

I glance around, wishing that someone else would enter the room so I didn't have to talk about my cancer with this girl who seems so calm about the tumors in her body. How can you be so carefree while your body is growing things that could kill you?

"I've got a tumor near my liver." I frown; that's the first time I've said it out loud since Doctor Barker gave us the news. "Not on my liver, though. My doctor is sure that surgery will take care of it and I can get back to my normal life."

"Which is?" she asks, curious.

"Dance," I say. "Ballet. I just auditioned for a studio in Paris, and that's where I'm planning to go in the fall."

"Wow, that's amazing. I'm a senior this year—well, I would be if I'd been going to school for the past two years. I'm almost done with all the work to finish my GED."

I nod, unsure of what to say. Doing homework feels like a waste of time when you're sick, like, what's the point? I said that once, the first time. It made Mom cry and Dad sat down next to me, with his face all serious, telling me how even though it felt like it, the cancer really wasn't going to last forever, that I needed to keep my brain sharp because when all of it was over, I'd be going back to school.

Now, though, I wish there was some way for me to keep dancing, to help me keep those skills up, so that I'll be ready for the Paris Academy when all of this is over. But with where the tumor is plus recovery from surgery, it'll be a few weeks, if not a month or two, before I can actually dance again the way I want to.

Lucy continues, "My tumors won't ever go away. We do surgeries when they get too big, mostly with the one on my brain. And the chemo helps slow the growth."

"Oh." I do not know how to talk to this girl.

"Yeah." She gives me another smile, which makes me feel slightly annoyed, because how can you be so happy when you have cancer? "They removed as much as they could two years ago when we first found it. Then last year, it started growing back, just like they said it would, and they did another surgery once it was big enough. But they won't ever be able to remove all of it because of the nerves it sits on. I'd become a vegetable. And I'd rather have a million surgeries than not be able to live my life."

I don't say what I think, which is that it doesn't sound like much of a life if you're stuck in the hospital all the time, trying to control a tumor that won't ever actually be cured.

"I just finished my first round of chemo, since on my last scan the tumor had started growing again. They're hoping that this helps slow it down."

"Wow." The word slips out of my mouth before I can think of a better response. "I mean, I'm so sorry, that does not sound fun."

Lucy nods. "I guess it's not exactly how I thought my last few years of high school would go. But, I believe there's a purpose for everything, so there's some purpose in this."

"Right," I say, but I don't believe that. How can all the bad things that happen in the world actually have a purpose? Couldn't we learn some of those lessons or whatever without all of the hard stuff? Or maybe different hard stuff that isn't quite so hard?

"So what about you?"

"What about me?"

Lucy is staring at me with an intensity that I'm not quite sure how to explain.

"What kind of cancer do you have?"

Oh. Just jumping right into this. I glance around the room as if looking for someone to save me from this conversation, but I'm stuck because no one else is around. "Lymphoma," I answer. "I had it when I was little. I was in remission for almost nine years."

"I'm so sorry," Lucy says, and then she surprises me; she reaches across the small distance between us and takes her hand in mine. "The diagnosis this time? Sorry if that's rude or nosy. I imagine we'll see each other a lot around here in the therapy group, but it helps to have friends."

To have friends who know what it's like, what you're going through. It's what she doesn't say, so I tell her again that it's just one tumor and that surgery should fix it. That I'll probably only be here once and that I'm not allowing myself to think of any other options. Which makes me feel a little selfish, now that I know her diagnosis.

When I finish, I blurt, "My best friend kissed me on Saturday." I wasn't ready to talk about that, but I am ready to be done talking about cancer.

Her eyes go wide in delight. "Oh, tell me all the details!"

I can't help but smile with her.

"Well," I say, unsure of where to start exactly. "I was kind of trying to date this other guy because I needed to focus on dance and my mom didn't want me to date Tucker—that's the guy I kissed. But she wanted me to date this other guy because I think she knew I didn't really like him, so he and I have been pretending to kind of date for half of the school year."

She giggles. "Wait, you fake dated another guy? And didn't fall in love with him?"

I let out a small laugh. I should have expected her to ask me questions about every single thing.

"Sort of fake dating, or fake whatever it is you are before a relationship. And I didn't fall in love with Shawn, he isn't the greatest guy. Plus..." I trail off.

"You like the other guy, the one you kissed?" she guesses.

"He's my best friend's cousin. We met a few years ago when he moved to be closer to LA; we live down in San Clemente. But anyway, he kissed me for the first time during the firework show on the Fourth of July last year and—"

Lucy interrupts, "How was that kiss?"

"Um, the best I've ever had?" I say it like a question, and she just laughs. And technically at that point, the only one I'd ever had.

"Go on," she urges.

I nod, biting my lip to hold back a grin. "So he kisses me last summer, right before I'm about to go to Paris for a six-week dance program at the school of my dreams. The whole first half, I couldn't stop thinking about him or about our kiss. It was so much of a distraction that even the instructors noticed. So I promised myself, and my mom, that I wouldn't date him."

"Wow, your life is so exciting," Lucy says.

I laugh. "Or incredibly dumb." I take a breath, and another person enters the room. Right, this is *group* therapy, I forgot. The boy sits at the edge of the semicircle and pulls out his phone, putting earbuds in his ears.

Lucy laughs, too. "Or maybe that."

"So, the night before I'm supposed to go home, one of my friends, Shawn, calls. We've known each other forever since his dad and my dad lived in the same apartment in college and are still good friends. It's so weird how most of my friends came from who my parents were friends with. Not the point of this story." I take a deep breath and continue.

"Shawn starts telling me about this girl, Libby, that he's desperately in love with"—I roll my eyes dramatically—"the same way he's desperately in love with a new girl every month, so I didn't really believe him when he told me that."

Lucy nods, watching me intently, hanging onto every word.

"Anyway, he's going on and on about how he loves her but how she'll never notice him, even though they're friends, but that she'll never notice him like *that,* like he wants her to. So I blurted out, 'why don't we fake date?'"

"You did not!?" Lucy gasps.

"I did, and for a few seconds I thought he might have hung up. But then he goes, 'you would do that for me?' And I said, 'it's not completely selfless, I need to get Tucker out of my head,' because we were friends and I could tell him that."

I let out another sigh. "But then, six months later, we were still fake dating, or fake whatever it was we were doing, since we never actually decided to be in a fake relationship. Our parents were thrilled. Mom encouraged it so much, and I didn't want to let her down. We never kissed. We only held hands if we had to, like if Tucker and Libby were around and we needed to pretend. I have a no PDA at school rule, so that was easy. But the more I got to actually know him, the less I liked him. I don't know if my friends even really believed it, but I saw the hurt every time Tucker really looked at me. I mean, on the surface he and I have been good friends like we've always been, but I knew I'd hurt him."

"Why go through all that?" Lucy asks quietly. "Isn't life already too short to ignore the things we actually want?"

Her words hit harder than they should and I don't reply. I'm realizing that now and I'm afraid we have wasted so much time already.

"I mean, now you get to be with Tucker, so something changed?" Lucy asks.

"My big audition was a couple of weeks ago, before I found out about all this." I gesture to my body. "But I haven't told him yet. He's a singer, I can't remember if I said that, but last weekend he sang a song to me in public and Shawn dumped me—well, fake dumped me? And then I told Tucker, and that's when we kissed. I want to be with him, to get a chance to be with him instead of running away from it." There, I said the words out loud. I can tell Tucker now, right?

"You need to tell him about the cancer," Lucy says.

I shake my head—this girl doesn't know me; she doesn't know my story, even if I've just shared a part of it. "I can't, not yet."

She gives my hand a gentle squeeze. "I get that," she says softly. "And sorry if what I just said was too much... I get like that sometimes. All up in everyone's business. Telling them what they should do."

"It's okay."

"I mean, not really." Lucy smiles at me as her nurse comes to check her IV that I only now realized she had. "Mom says it's probably because I'm dying, but I'm always urging people to be honest and just live their lives, since life's too short to do anything other than that."

I wait for her words to sink in, but they don't. Because sure, I've got cancer, but I've still got plenty of time. I'm not worried about dying. I still have the time to be with Tucker like I want to. I just wish I could have realized it sooner so we could have had *more* time together. Like he said, senior year could have been our year.

"I get that," I say. Or at least, I want to get it. I want to be brave and tell Tucker how I feel, I want to stop wasting time. But we're going to have to say goodbye when I go to Paris, so will it be worth the heartbreak?

Lucy's next smile doesn't quite reach her eyes. It's as if she's pretending, too, as if she knows that I don't believe her, that I don't think that life is too short. Because it still feels like I have all the time in the world, so why not wait a little longer to tell him the truth about my cancer and my feelings?

We have to stop talking after that because three more people join us; one of them is the therapist, who starts to explain how group therapy works.

I listen the whole time.

It was nice talking to Lucy about everything, but I'm not quite ready to share everything with a roomful of strangers. Especially when all of my feelings are jumbled anyway.

Lucy hugs me before I leave. It's a little awkward, since she's still a stranger, but I give her a smile and turn to go find Dad. As I walk out of the hospital, my heart fills with an emotion I can't quite name.

It's not until we're almost home that what I feel is relief—relief that I'm not alone in this, that I have a friend who knows what I'm going through, because as of now, Lucy is my newest friend. Or at least something close to it.

"What was that look?" Nathan asks as soon as the warning bells go off in my head, telling me I shouldn't be friends with Lucy, that we both have cancer and this might not end well.

"What look?"

"Well, you were smiling one second, then the next you looked like someone died."

"No one died," I snap.

"I didn't say that anyone did." When Nathan looks at me, I feel like he can see right through me, right into my mind.

"Right, I know." I'm trying to brush it off, wondering how I'll avoid Lucy the next time we run into each other when Dad glances back at us.

"Who was that girl you were talking to today?" he asks. "When I peeked in the window, you were talking to a girl sitting next to you."

Swallow, I tell myself. *It's going to be fine. You can be friends with the girl who has cancer. You* are *the girl who has cancer.* "Her name is Lucy and she was very friendly."

"Well," Dad says, "that'll be nice, to have a familiar face now when you're there."

I nod, but can't say anything else. Suddenly, I can't breathe. I can't say that she's been living surgery to surgery, but it's too dangerous to have that many surgeries on her brain so often. Chemo will slow the growth of her tumor down, but death is at the end of the barrel she's looking down. *Being friends with her isn't a good idea,* I think, because what's the point if in a few months she'll be gone; why would I want that hurt in my life?

It's a selfish thought, but I think it anyway. Promising myself I will ask to be seated away from Lucy next time if she's in the clinic. I don't want to get attached to her if she's just going to be gone soon after the next time I see her.

11

"YOU READY FOR THIS?" Nathan asks as we get out of the car and head up the walk to the front door.

"Ready to watch *Bambi* for the millionth time? Sure."

"No. " Nathan looks at me pointedly. "You can't keep this a secret, Rosie."

"Just a little longer," I promise. I'm not ready to talk about my tumor or the surgery. Tonight is the first night I'm hanging out with Tucker since our kiss. And even though Nathan is my twin, I still haven't told anyone about the kiss. I guess I'm just in a secret-keeping mood. I'm trying to process everything, and I'm not ready to share my heart. Plus, I'm not sure how to act tonight. Do I sit by Tucker? Will he hold my hand? Do I want him to? I do want him to. I just want to be us for a little longer, without me being the girl who has cancer again. It's easier this way—people can't treat me differently if they don't know.

Nathan shakes his head and knocks on the door. It swings open almost immediately, revealing Kenny, one of Grace's younger brothers.

"Oh, it's just you two," he groans, and then runs back down the hallway.

"Hey, I thought you liked us." Nathan steps into the house as Micah, Grace's other brother, comes running down the hall.

"It wasn't the pizza," Kenny says, and Micah's face falls, too.

"You made us excited."

"Sorry," we say at the same time.

"Everyone is downstairs," Micah says and heads back down the hall, head hanging low.

"That kid sure loves pizza," my brother says as he slips off his shoes. I nod and follow him down to the basement, which already smells like popcorn. Grace is sitting on the couch in the dim room, the light of her phone making her face bright.

"Hey," I say. She grins up at me. Nathan plops onto the couch next to her, pulling her phone from her hands.

"Hey! I was looking at that, but I am happy you're here." She tries to reach for her phone, but Nathan tosses it onto the beanbag. Our movie nights are supposed to be phone-free—a decision she made without the rest of us—yet she's the one who ignores the rule most of the time.

"Tucker will probably be down in a minute," she says, just as I hear him come down the stairs. I turn to face him for the first time since I ran out of his dressing room last week. I mean, yes, I have seen him at school. But this is different and we both know it.

"Hi." I pull on the hem of my shirt, unsure of what to do with my hands.

"Hi." Tucker stares at me, then glances in Nathan's direction. "Hey."

"Hello," Nathan says, looking between the two of us, confusion all over his face.

Grace jumps up and appears by my side. "Is this a Jess and Rory moment?" My cheeks turn pink.

"A what?" Tucker asks, looking more confused than Nathan.

"Tucker kissed me on Saturday," I blurt and all three pairs of eyes turn toward me. "And Shawn told me he didn't want to date."

Grace's eyes go wide. "Before or after the kiss?"

"Before."

"And the two of you kissed?" She gestures between me and Tucker and I still feel his eyes on me, but I can't bring myself to look at him yet. I'm hot all over. This wasn't how I thought tonight would go.

"Yes," I say, sounding much calmer than I actually feel.

"So this *is* a Jess and Rory moment!" Grace jumps up and down a little as she says it, as if she's been hoping for this to happen.

"I guess so," I tell her.

"Um," Tucker says. "What does that even mean?"

Grace rolls her eyes. "He'll never know about our other true love." Then to Tucker, she says, "If you know, you know." He kind of shrugs, still waiting for her to explain. It's kind of cute that he doesn't get her *Gilmore Girls* reference. But if she's not going to explain, then neither am I.

"Wait," I say, because she said our *other* true love. "What is our first love?"

"Dance for you, Disney for me," she says. "Now I'm going to sit, because standing here in this circle is kind of weird."

"And me," Tucker says suddenly, and we all look at him. Grace raises her eyebrows and even though this moment feels like it shouldn't be funny, I almost start laughing. What is he talking about?

"And you what?" Nathan asks and I let out a giggle. Grace's cheek twitches.

"I'm one of your true loves." Tucker says it confidently, his eyes not leaving mine, and I know my cheeks are red.

"Um, no," Grace says, grabbing my hand and pulling me to follow her onto the couch. "You probably don't even make the top five... the ocean has to fit in there somewhere."

I nod in agreement. "But you, um, do make the list..." Did I just say that out loud?

"I'll just sing for you again." He winks. "That seems to do

something to ya." Without another word, he sits next to me, our arms and legs touching, but he doesn't reach for my hand.

"Oo, he's good," Grace says.

"Of course I am. I'm Tucker Bensen and everyone falls in love with me," he says sarcastically. Nathan smacks him with a pillow and we all laugh.

After *Bambi* is done, we head upstairs to see if there is any pizza left. Grace tells Nathan she has an outfit that she wants his opinion on and they head off in the direction of her bedroom.

"So," I say, looking at Tucker, who's already watching me.

So," he says back. He's leaning against the counter and there's a part of me that wants to move closer and kiss him, but my body seems to be rooted to the spot.

"I have something to show you," he says suddenly, grabbing my hand and pulling me through the house and to his makeshift bedroom. I think it was technically an old storage space, since there isn't a window. His bed has been shoved into the corner, and on the opposite end of the room is a large dresser.

"I don't think I've ever been in your room before," I say as I take it all in. Even though it's cramped, it's tidy.

"Uh, yeah." He runs a hand through his hair, then motions to the bed. "Sit, please."

"Oh-kay," I say slowly. I sit on his bed and lean against his pillows, which smell like him—pine and spearmint. I close my eyes and inhale again.

My heart speeds up as I open my eyes. He is leaning down to open his guitar case. There's a crash from somewhere in the house and then somewhat muffled voices of Micah and Kenny yelling at each other.

He closes the door so it's only opened a crack. "Never a dull moment here," he says sheepishly and runs a hand through his hair again, like he's nervous.

"I like it," I say honestly, because I do love it here. Even with dance, I spent so much of my childhood here. "My house is far too quiet all the time."

"Yeah, I don't really remember quiet. Someone is always making noise here." He sits on the edge of his bed, across from me, and pulls his guitar into his lap.

"How do you even think?" I ask as there's another thud from somewhere above us, this time followed by laughter. "How do you write songs?"

"No idea." Tucker smiles. "I think I just got used to it." He's been living in this cramped room for over two years. "And I use noise-cancelling headphones," he adds with a laugh.

"It's kinda comforting, ya know, knowing you're not ever alone."

"Sometimes." He laughs. "Sometimes being alone is needed."

"Well, you're always welcome at my house. Of course, my mom might kill you, but you're still welcome, from me anyway."

"Thanks," he says, strumming his guitar and then tuning it. "Now, I'm going to sing before I chicken out."

I nod, not trusting my voice. The words are on the tip of my tongue and I know that Nathan is right; I have to tell him that my cancer is back. I should tell him before he sings, but selfishly, I don't want to ruin this moment.

"I've never had a girl on my bed before, or in my room," he says as his hand hovers over the strings.

"Well, if it makes you feel better, I've never been on a guy's bed before," I say. His cheeks go dark. We're watching each other now; this is part of the dance. I just want him to come out and say how he actually feels, instead of all this skirting around. Even with our kiss, we haven't actually talked about how we feel. I know he likes me—from what he's said in the past—but I want him to actually say it again, so I can tell him I feel the same way.

Instead of sharing his feelings he says, "Well, I guess that makes me one lucky guy." His eyes never leave mine. "I'm really going to sing now, because I've always been able to express myself better with music. This is another cover, the song I've been writing isn't quite ready."

I nod again, still not sure what to say. I want to ask what it means—why he's writing me a song—and I've already heard him sing and I know I love his voice. But this time, it's a show just for me.

He closes his eyes and starts to play, and it's a song I know I've never heard before. I watch as his face relaxes as he loses himself in the music, just like I do when I'm dancing.

Then he starts singing.

I'm a puddle by the time he's done.

Mush.

Fallen.

Fell.

Hard.

For him. His voice. His face. Everything.

I might even be in love.

I'm smiling and I'm crying.

He finally opens his eyes, and he takes me in when he sees my tears. I'm in his arms in an instant.

"I loved it," I say, my tears falling silently onto his shirt.

"I, um"—he clears his throat—"I didn't expect you to cry."

"That's not why I'm crying," I tell him, leaning back. He brushes away a tear with his thumb.

"Why then?"

"Why did you choose that song?" I ask instead.

"Because it makes me think of you," he says, his brow furrowed in confusion.

"Why?" I ask. I know the answer; deep down, I really do. But I need him to say it. He needs to actually say it. He needs to say it before I tell him.

Please say it. I'm having a hard time breathing.

"I like you, Rosie, I like you a lot. You have to know that."

"I think I like you, too," I say honestly and he laughs a little. My heart is breaking into a million tiny pieces.

"You think? I feel like this is a flashback to the first time I told you I liked you, all those years ago." He's smiling, though, as we both remember the moment.

I nod. "Well, okay, maybe more than think. I know. I like you, too."

He grins and gives me a hug, even though I'm already in his arms.

"So why were you crying?" he asks, and I'm not brave. I can't say the words. Because saying them out loud makes it too real, and I'm not ready for that yet. I was able to say the words to Lucy, but she was a stranger. This is Tucker.

"Um, right," I say, my mind is whirling, trying to come up with a good enough excuse. "I'm just sad that here we are talking about how we feel and I'll be going to Paris in the fall. But, I mean, that's silly to even assume we'd be together that long..."

He shifts, moving me closer to him and cutting me off. His eyes drop down to my lips, which I lick nervously. His eyes go dark.

I have cancer.

I have cancer.

I have cancer! It's back and I have to have surgery soon. That's what I want to scream and shout and tell him, but instead, I lean forward so he can kiss me.

It will be the first time that I'm actually ready for it. And boy, am I ready for it.

The door bangs open and I fly back. "There you two are, ready for another movie?" Grace asks and she's got a grin on her face.

"We'll be down in a second." He sighs, never taking his eyes off me.

"Now, please? You can make out later," she says. I know my cheeks are red as I stand. Tucker gets up, too, and holds my hand.

"Later?" he asks.

"Later," I promise, praying harder than I ever have to a God I'm not sure I believe in that we get a lot more laters and trying to ingrain every moment of tonight in my mind so I can write about it in my journal later.

I started writing in my journal actively the first time I had cancer. Doctor Barker said it would help me feel a bit better if I could get some of my thoughts out on paper, but even when the cancer was gone, I didn't stop writing. It's messy and imperfect, but I guess in a way it helps me make sense of everything. Even if it's the only place I've really been truthful about my feelings for the past several years.

journal entries from junior year

AUGUST 4

Dear Journal,

It's been over a year since I wrote in this journal. I'm about to start my junior year. This year is big in my dance career, in that I'll spend the next 16 months training hard for my audition to the Paris Academy. Next summer, I'll get to go to their 6-week intensive summer program that's exclusively for students who will be seniors when school starts.

That's only 11 months away, and I can't wait.

So. What's happened since I last wrote?

Grace and Leo broke up (again), and she thought it was the end of her fairy tale romance, that she'd never get a chance at love again. I binge-watched every Pixar movie with her three times. There were lots of tears (those movies are sad) and lots of ice cream. Then, one day Grace shows up at my door with the news that Leo asked her to prom AND to be his girlfriend again. So they're together again, and stronger than ever? She keeps asking me if she seems happier than when she was with him before, and I guess she seems happier. She just seems a little obsessed with love, if you ask me.

Then there's Tucker, who seems to be just as obsessed with love and romance as Grace is.

Just. Not with me.

Idk why that hurts so much to write. We both decided that we're really good as friends, that we shouldn't date. (Plus, there's the fact that my mom would probably kill both of us...) but. It still really hurt when he told us he was going out with Amber Monroe, Missy Esplin's best friend (aka the girl who's been mean to me forever—Missy, not Amber). They make a pretty cute couple, but it still sucks every time I see them together, even though I pretend it doesn't.

Cause I'm not supposed to like him, remember? I even got to the point where I told him I don't. And I guess I don't, but kind of do? I'm not really sure what my feelings are at this point. He's my very best friend and I'd die without him in my life. He's been gone most of the summer, performing at state fairs and carnivals and things, but every time he's in town he hangs out with Amber (which is fair, she's his girlfriend) and she's always posting photos of them together.

He hasn't ever posted one of them though, so it probably makes me a bad person, but that kind of makes me secretly a little happy, since the last picture he posted on Instagram was of me (well, and Grace and Nathan) but still not of him and his girlfriend.

Grace told me that he told her that Amber said I love you to him a few weeks ago, but that he didn't say it back.

Idk what that means either. He seems like the type of guy who would say that to a girl he was dating, since he's all about happily ever afters and stuff (seriously, he's just like Grace in that way).

But I wonder why he hasn't said it. I can't ask him, cause that would make me... come off as, idk what... but I can't ask him.

I'm not sure how ready I am to see them at school together all the time. They've only been together over the summer. Will she eat lunch with us? Or hang out with us? She doesn't really hang with us now, but could that change???

All these questions and feelings are so dumb.

August 30

Dear Journal,

Tucker and Amber broke up.

I feel guilty for how happy that makes me. I'm truly a terrible person. I won't be with him, but I don't want him to be with anyone else...

September 14

Dear Journal,

Everything is back to normal (well, friendship normal) and I'm glad. Tucker was never really gone (I mean, he was when he was singing in different places around the state) but I feel like I got my best friend back.

October 31

Dear Journal,

I came to school dressed up as Catwoman (Grace's idea for all of us to go as superheroes) and Tucker came as Batman. I am 110% sure that she did this on purpose.

Later, at the beach party Grace hosted, she said we looked like a cute couple with a cute couples costume.

Tucker's face went so red. I'm sure mine did, too.

Neither of us said anything about her comment. We just kind of ignored it and then went down to the beach when her party was over to listen to the waves at midnight.

January 11

Dear Journal,

I officially have less than a year until my Paris audition. But... that's not what I want to write about.

I'm not sure my heart will be able to take it. Whenever Tucker smiles at me, or even just glances in my direction, my heart skips a beat.

I will not let him be a distraction.

I will not let him be a distraction.

I will not let him be a distraction.

I do wonder what he kisses like, though.

No.

I will not let him be a distraction.

End of story.

April 3

Dear Journal,

Tucker asked Amber to prom when I told him I wasn't interested in going.

Why why why why why?

July 4

Dear Journal,

AHHHHHHHHH!!!!!!!!!!!!!!

Okay. Okay, before I freak out, let me back up a little bit.

I haven't written in this journal in a few months. Our spring concert was AMAZING and I've just been dancing or working at the studio most of the summer. And going to Disneyland every now and then with Grace when she goes (okay, not every time she goes, because she's been going almost every day lately).

Today marks the end of summer for me. On Monday, I'll fly with Mom and Dad to Paris for my six-week intensive. I am SOOOO excited!

I wasn't thinking about that at all today. Today deserved my full attention. Grace, who loves this day and our traditions almost as much as I do, wore a red jumpsuit with a blue belt, and all white accessories.

Today is the Fourth of July. My all-time favorite holiday. It's not even my favorite because it's Independence Day (because let's be real here… sometimes this country isn't worth celebrating.) It's my favorite because we've been doing the same things with my family every single year since I was born and that's what makes it special. I LOVE traditions.

The lame parade that we watch every year. The hours of food and picnicking at Grace's house. How we almost always end up soaking wet in our clothes because we jump in the ocean when we get too hot, and we never bring swimsuits.

And of course, ending the night on the pier or the beach, watching the fireworks.

This year was no different.

I got up early to get ready. Nathan helped me braid red ribbon into my hair and I wore my new blue and white dress that Mom got me a few weeks ago with my red shoes. What? I like being festive even when I don't really feel festive.

The parade went off as usual. There was a kid next to us that was so sad every time a float went by. I think she didn't understand that we don't get to be in the parade, just watch.

My parents prepped their portion of the picnic (watermelon and a pasta salad) before we headed over to Grace's for the bbq.

Tucker just smiled and shook his head when he saw us, but he did wear a red shirt (I think Grace made him).

As always, Erin threw the best party. There was so much food to eat and all the little kids were playing and running around. Pretty much everyone on the street stopped by at some point. Even Tucker's mom was in town visiting. She's really nice.

Yesterday, I told Grace that I have feelings for Tucker. She did her usual squeal when I told her, but I told her that I was just getting it out of my system, that I really need to focus on ballet until January, and after that I can do a little less, but I really need to train for my audition.

She said I was being dumb, because it was 'obvious how he feels' but I just told her not to say anything. He dated Amber off and on all last school year, so I don't know how 'obvious' it really is about how he feels about me. He hasn't told me that he likes me since that first time.

She didn't tell him, but she kept making these faces at me that I KNOW he could see... like kissy faces and wiggling (waggling?) her eyebrows whenever I was by Tucker. Which was a lot since we're friends... thankfully, he didn't ask about her weird looks or even mention it; probably because he's used to all of her weird antics.

The afternoon is all kind of a blur to me, even though it was just a few hours ago. We ended up in the ocean at some point, just like always. Nathan was telling dumb dad jokes while we sat on the beach in the sun, but we were all dying of laughter because even though they were dumb, they were still funny.

Then it was time for the firework show. We headed to the beach, just off the pier, with blankets in hand just like we always do.

I ended up sitting right next to Tucker on the small blanket that Grace had grabbed for the four of us. Him, me, Nathan, and Grace. Nathan and Grace were in their own little world, talking about college, Disney, and who knows what else.

Tucker bumped his leg with mine (!!!!) and he said "Cozy, eh?" I know I blushed, but thankfully it was dark, so I don't think he noticed.

"Very," I said.

THEN he said, "But, it gives me an excuse to touch you." And he just left his leg by mine the rest of the night.

When the firework show started, his fingers brushed mine (!!!!) and I started to wonder what it'd really be like to hold his hand.

THEN. THEN. Oh my gosh THEN he whispered, "I've got a secret." So I turned to look at him. His face was blue and red, reflecting the light of the fireworks. He was looking at me like he never had before.

AND THEN HE KISSED ME!!!

It was over so fast.

(Does that make me sound needy?)

But one second his lips were on mine, and the next it was just a memory; the faint smell of his mint gum still lingering in the air. When I opened my eyes, he was looking at me, and I said, "That was a good secret."

And then he just smiled and looked back at the fireworks!

We didn't talk about it. He didn't even hug me goodnight when we left... he just kissed me and then went on as if life was just normal and that kissing each other was a regular part of our days!

I want him to kiss me again.

No. I want to ask him what the kiss meant.

No. I need to tell him that nothing can happen. Not until after my audition.

Gosh I'm going to remember this kiss forever.

Why did he have to kiss me now? Why did it have to be so perfect (even if it was short?) Why couldn't he have waited?

What if this messes everything up?

12

IT'S MONDAY, and my surgery is in eleven days. Grace and I are passing notes in math class, because it's test review day. Not that we're reviewing for a test, nope. Today we're supposed to be going over the test we took before Christmas break so we can understand what we did wrong on the problems we missed.

So. When do you think Tuck's gonna ask you to the Valentine's Dance?

Prom is big pretty much everywhere, but for some reason, the Valentine's Dance is the big event at our school; it always has been. Grace's question fills my stomach with butterflies.

You mean if he asks...

He's going to ask you, Rosie. He's in love with you.

This is the moment I should tell her; tell her that I will technically still be in recovery from surgery when the dance is, but I can't tell her in a note, and I'm not going to tell her yet. I just want things to be normal, at least until I hear back from Paris. Doctor Barker is confident that with the surgery and monitoring me, maybe I'll be able to dance with PBA in September. I have to be able to go though; I'm willing that into existence, as Grace would say.

I just hope he asks soon.

He will.

I hope so.

Tucker pokes my back with a pencil and when Mrs. Adams looks down, I turn to face him. His eyes flick to the note folded on the edge of his desk and I grab it, unfolding it as quietly as possible. There's a usual hum of chatter in the classroom, and like always, it completely covers the rustle of paper.

ROSIE—
WILL YOU.....
COME OVER AFTER SCHOOL?
CIRCLE YES OR NO.
— TUCKER

I know I shouldn't be disappointed. I want more than a note asking me to the dance, but I still deflate slightly when I read his note. Then I circle yes and discreetly turn back to return the note to him.

I feel like we don't write notes as much as we used to. Not just me and Tucker, but in general. We did a lot in elementary school.

Then by middle school, almost everyone had a phone, so texting was easier than writing a note. But I like the finality of a note. That when you write it, it's there forever. I mean, I guess that's sort of how texts are, too, but it still feels different. It's something tangible that I can keep.

It's why I still keep a journal, to get my thoughts out on paper in a real way. It's helped since I had cancer the first time, and maybe it will help this time, too. I keep writing my note to Grace.

Disney movie after school?

DUH. But it won't be right after school. I'm staying after to help Nathan study for his chemistry test.

That's fine. I'm going to hang out with Tucker, after my mandatory hour at the dance studio.

You still haven't told your mom that you hate working there, have you?

No. :/ I don't know how to now. She thinks that because I love dancing, I also love manning the front desk one hour a day.

You should tell her you hate it. That you'd rather be dancing, she'd understand that. I could tell her for you.

HA. Thanks, but no. I think I need to be the one to tell her. I just don't know how.

Not that it matters right now since Doctor Barker made me promise I'd take it easy because my energy will be low and there are going to be days when I physically won't be able to dance at all. All I'll be able to do is man the front desk at the studio. But I don't tell her that.

You should still tell her.

I nod in response because Mrs. Adams stands back up at the front of the class, reminding us that there may or may not be another pop quiz next class.

The final bell rings and I fold the note and put it in my notebook, grabbing my backpack.

Tucker takes my hand as soon as we're in the hallway. A jolt of energy shoots through me as our fingers wrap around each other. I'm still not used to this; to being his girlfriend or holding his hand in public. We haven't had the conversation about being girlfriend and boyfriend, but I don't think we need to since we both know that's what this is.

But, I did hear Amber telling Libby last week that it was tacky of me to already be dating Tucker, even though things just ended with Shawn. I didn't hear what Libby had to say about that, but I'm not sure she was mad about the breakup. I've seen them making out after school in his car, so I think things are going just fine.

We say goodbye to Grace and Nathan, and walk down the nearly empty hall, past the gym that leads to the parking lot. Right before we get outside, Tucker pauses and kisses me.

We've only been together for a week and already this is a habit. Not many people use this hallway, as no one has gym last period, and since our classroom is right by it, we're usually the first ones out of the school. He always stops and kisses me though. They're quick kisses, ones that leave me wanting more, but it's really our only time alone.

"So, I have to work at the studio for an hour before we can hang out," I say after he kisses me one last time before heading out into the bright sun.

"I know. Want me to pick you up after?" He grabs his keys from his pocket and unlocks his truck.

"Yup, that'd be good, considering Nathan has to work today and is taking the car," I tell him.

He nods. "Great." Then, once we're in the car, looking for a song to listen to, he says, "Murphy called me last night."

"Wait, what?" I feel a little like Grace when I let out a small squeal and he laughs.

"Yeah."

"Well?" He cannot just leave me hanging like this.

"I'm opening for Peyton Matthews in the fall"—I lean over and hug him—"and I'm meeting with a label this weekend to talk about my first album."

"What? No way!" I grin. "That's fantastic, Tuck!"

He grabs my hand as we pull out of the parking lot. "I was hoping you'd come up to the studio with me?"

"I'd love to," I say, grateful I'll still have one week before my surgery so I can enjoy this with him.

"Awesome." He grins and we both smile all the way to the ballet studio.

Tucker is thirteen minutes late to pick me up.

"What have you been up to?" I ask him when he finally pulls up to the dance studio. It was a slow hour, since most of the classes don't even start until after three, but Mom wants there to be someone at the desk all the time.

"Nothing much," he answers, but he won't look at me and I know him well enough to know that he's keeping a secret from me.

"What's going on?" I ask him on the way to his house.

"Huh? Nothing," he says, avoiding my gaze. It's a good thing I'm the one with a tumor, because it looks like I'm better than he is when it comes to keeping secrets.

"Is that why you won't look at me?" I tease and he finally looks at me when we pull up to a stoplight.

"I'm looking at you," he says, and his eyes are as blue as the ocean today.

"Okay, but you weren't." I narrow my eyes. "What are you hiding?"

"Nothin'," he says again. "Just thinking about next week and my album. That's why I was late, I was working on a new song."

He could be telling the truth, but I get the feeling there's more to the story.

"Oh yeah? What's this one about?" I ask, instead of pushing him for more.

"You."

I shove his shoulder. "Liar."

"No, really, it's about you," he says, glancing at me.

"Oh, well, can I hear it soon?" I ask him. He's joked about writing songs about me before, but I don't know for sure if he ever has or not.

"Maybe."

"Oh, come on. It's about me, after all," I whine.

He just smiles. "Maybe."

"You could play it for me when we get to your house since we might have to wait for Grace."

"We'll see." He says it in a way that sounds more like no than yes. We pull into the driveway and Grace comes bouncing down the front walk.

"You got lucky," I tell him, and he just gives me a small smile. "This time."

"I'll play it for you, at some point," he says, and then squeezes my hand three times.

I squeeze his hand back.

Later, when Tucker drops me off at home, the house is quiet. It means Dad is still at his art show, Mom's probably still at the studio, and Nathan is still working. I grab an apple and a granola bar before heading upstairs. I pause when I reach the landing and notice my bedroom door is shut, which is weird, because I usually leave it open.

I tentatively open the door and let out a small gasp at what I see. There are hundreds of pink, red, and purple hearts covering my bed and the floor.

The biggest heart on my bed says, "Will you go to the Valentine's Dance with me? - Tucker." I let out a giddy laugh and clap my hands. I send a photo to Grace.

GRACE

FINALLY!!! Now we really need to get your dress ready!

Did you know he was doing this today??

Maybe. Maybe not ;)

How should I answer???

Should I give a cute answer?

Why is our school so weird? Why do we make a bigger deal out of this than prom?

IDK. Because we want to be special? You could answer with a song? He'd probably love that...

UGH. He asked so cute. Now I have to be cute back.

> That's an idea for sure… we'll see though.

He did ask cute. You do need to be cute back.

> Tell me about it.

> Did Leo ask you?

Three dots appear then disappear. I wonder what she's typing.

I'm not going with Leo.

> What? But you are still going, right? You said you'd make our dresses.

My mind is spinning. I thought for sure Leo would ask her again and that they'd be together for the rest of the year. I guess I was wrong.

I'm still going, just not with Leo. And I'm making our dresses. They're nearly done.

She's been making costumes to wear at Disneyland for years, so when she offered ages ago to make our dresses for the Valentine's Dance, I said yes. At the time, I told myself that even though I'd probably be at the dance with Shawn, at least I'd have a pretty dress. But now I get a pretty dress and I get to go with Tucker.

I know u secretly like all the cute stuff that T does for you.

> OK. So maybe I do like the cute things he does. And I'm not dropping the dance subject. Who are you going with??

That's a secret.

But here, I found this <link to article about ways to answer to prom>

SECRET?? I'm your best friend!

It's a secret.

When she doesn't send anything else, I type out another reply.

Thanks for the link, but WHY ARE THERE A MILLION WAYS TO ANSWER???

¯_(ツ)_/¯

NOT HELPFUL.

LUUUV YOOOU.

If you really loved me, you'd tell me who you're going to the dance with.

She leaves me on read.

13

"CAN I COME WITH YOU?" Grace asks when I get out of the car. I have one week until my surgery, which she and Tucker still don't know about. But today isn't about me, today is about Tucker.

"You should be asking Tucker that question," I say, wondering why she was waiting for me outside.

"He's been avoiding me all morning." She sticks out her tongue like she does when she gets annoyed.

"Maybe he doesn't want you to come?" I ask. I'm not trying to be rude, but today is a big deal for him. He gets to officially meet Peyton Matthews and play a few songs for her before he can open for her in the fall on her stadium tour.

"But you want me to come, right?" She asks me, and for the first time, I feel conflicted. Grace has always been one of my best friends, and she has always come first for me, no ifs ands or buts, and I don't want to become the girl who puts her boyfriend above her best friend. But this, having her tag along today, really isn't up to me.

"You need to ask him," I say again, heading toward the front door. I trip over the small dip in her front walk, like I almost always do, but catch myself before I fall completely on my face.

"For a ballerina, you're pretty clumsy." I look up at the sound of Tucker's voice. It's been an ongoing joke since well, forever, that even though I'm graceful on the dance floor, I'm pretty much a walking disaster anywhere else.

"That's true," I say with a smile and give him a big hug. "You ready for today?"

He nods, looking over my head toward Grace. "You can come," he says and she claps. "But you have to promise to be quiet when we're at the studio, both of you."

I nod; I already knew this part. Murphy said I could come as long as I wasn't in the way or loud.

We climb into his truck, and it's got a bench seat which means I get to sit right next to him the whole ride up to LA. I pick the music—the playlist of songs that Tucker said reminded him of us —and we settle in for the mostly quiet ride. I can tell that he's nervous by the way he grips the steering wheel and how he doesn't try to keep the conversation going when it fades out like he usually does. He keeps one of his hands in mine, though, for the entire ride.

When we pull into the parking lot, Grace hops out of the car, but I tug on Tucker's hand before he gets out.

"Yeah?" he asks.

"It's gonna be fine," I promise him, even though I have no idea how these things work or if it actually will be fine.

"I know," he replies, but his jaw is tight, like he doesn't quite believe me. I can't tell if he's just nervous or if something else is happening in his head.

Murphy welcomes us into the studio and puts Grace and I in a room with a window facing another part of the studio and tells us to be quiet. We can hear everything that's happening in the other room.

"This is so exciting," she whispers, and I nod, not trusting myself to speak. I've still only seen and heard him sing a handful of times, so that's not why I'm nervous. Some of his nervous energy must be getting to me and I'm on edge, waiting for disaster to strike.

It doesn't though. Tucker warms up before Peyton gets there, and when she walks in the room, everyone seems to light up. From what I can tell, she's friendly and excited to hear him in person.

"I saw a video of you a few weeks ago, and I told my manager, 'He's the one.'" When she tells him this, he grins and just shakes his head, embarrassed.

Then he plays for her—two covers, and one original. The original isn't about me, but it's good.

When he's finished singing, Grace and I are invited in to meet Peyton. My best friend seems a little awestruck, even though I didn't know before today that she even liked country music. Maybe it's just because she's never really been in the same room as a famous person? I haven't either, unless you count famous ballerinas—most of the world doesn't. I know Peyton is talented, but she's also just a person.

"I'm really looking forward to having you on tour with me," Peyton tells Tucker as he's packing up his guitar.

"I'm really excited," he says, full of enthusiasm.

"Yeah," she says. "When your dad first suggested it, I wasn't sure what to think. I'd never even heard of you, ya know?" Peyton doesn't seem to notice how Tucker freezes at the mention of his dad. "But then I looked you up and just knew that I had to have you on tour with me. It's gonna be big, for both of us. I won't be surprised if you have a record deal before the tour even starts."

"Right," he says in a stiff voice, but Peyton doesn't notice.

"Anyway, great to meet you! Can't wait till rehearsals start," she says in a way that makes me feel like she's our age, instead of the same age as our parents.

"Yup," is all Tucker seems to be able to manage. "See you at rehearsals." Then Peyton leaves the room and he sinks down onto one of the plush red couches, burying his face in his hands.

"Okay, that went well," Murphy starts, still looking at her phone—the woman rarely glances up at him—so I'm surprised when she does now. She can tell right away that something is off with Tucker. "What is it?"

He doesn't reply. I sit beside him and rub his back in a way I hope is comforting. Grace is frozen in the corner.

"What's going on?" Murphy asks again.

"His dad," I say at the same time he puts his head in his hands and says, "My dad."

Murphy looks at us expectantly.

"He's the whole reason I got this gig," he mutters, his voice muffled because he hasn't pulled his head out of his hands.

"Right," Murphy says tentatively.

"Wait," I say, staring at her. "You knew the whole time?"

Tucker's head snaps up at this.

Murphy gives a little shrug. "Of course I knew, and of course he's the reason you got this gig. Peyton Matthews is a big name. Touring with her doesn't just happen because she came across your video."

"I don't need his help," he spits.

"Doesn't matter." Murphy shrugs again. "You got it and now you're going on tour."

"No," he says. "Ugh." He stands and throws his fist up in the air, like he's trying to punch something but only comes up with air. "There has to be another way, a different tour."

Murphy shakes her head, then smiles. "There's not, but your dad wasn't here today. I've had interactions with Peyton before, and she's not all that friendly. She genuinely likes you. You should be grateful."

"I am," he says, rubbing his hands behind his neck. "I'm just pissed, too. I wanted to do this on my own. I didn't want his help."

Murphy looks at him as if she doesn't believe him.

"I just want to prove that I can do this without having his push or pull. Almost no one knows he's my dad."

"He's a big name, Tucker. Sometimes getting your foot in the door is all about who you know. You should be glad he put your name out there."

"He's not getting a thank you card," he mutters. Then he shakes his head. "I'm beat, let's get out of here."

Grace finally moves from the corner, grabbing her bag and walking out without a word.

"Why is she acting so weird?" I ask Tucker as we follow her out into the bright sun.

"No idea," he says. "But if I had to guess, it'd be that she hates my dad almost as much as I do."

"Why?" Even though he told me about his dad and what happened, Grace has never mentioned it. We've never talked about it together, and until this moment, I didn't know she had any feelings on the topic.

"He's not really a person people like, you know that much. And she's fiercely loyal, so if someone hurts the people she loves, she doesn't play nice after that."

I nod, knowing this is true. I know this about my best friend, but I've been trying not to think about all the good things Grace is lately, because it'll break her when she finds out I have a tumor and didn't tell her.

But it will be gone in a week, and everything will be fine. I nod in agreement with my own silent thought. This will all be over soon.

"I should have known he had something to do with this." He hits the side of his truck. "I mean, I should have guessed why this was happening, why it seemed too good to be true that Peyton Matthews wants me to open for her."

"You're good, anyone can see that," I try.

He just shakes his head. "He'll just hold this over me forever, that he was good enough to make it on his own when he was seventeen, but that I needed his help to get going at eighteen."

"That's not true," I say. "And you know it. You moved out here about to close on a record deal. It didn't work out, and that's okay. You got here because of who *you* are, not because of anything he did."

"I mean, he's sort of the reason you're here," Grace says and we both look at her. "I mean, on Earth, not at the studio. He's your dad. But he wasn't around, he's always been a jerk to pretty much every single person. So yeah, maybe he's the biggest jerk on the planet, but he still put your name out there."

He smiles slightly at this.

"He's such a jerk," he says. "And he's still not getting a thank you card, but I am opening for Peyton Matthews." His mood shifts so suddenly, I'm not sure how or what changed. One second he was mad that his dad played a role in this, but now he's back to being in awe about this twist of fate. He's finally going on tour. Opening for one of the biggest country singers. It is a big deal.

"Yeah, you are!" I reach over and squeeze his hand, and he squeezes back.

"You'll come to the first show, before you leave for Paris?" he asks tentatively.

I can't help but grin. "I wouldn't miss it for the world."

He presses a kiss against my forehead before letting me go.

The whole way home, the words are on the tip of my tongue. *My cancer is back. I have a tumor, but I'm going to be okay. I just didn't want you to worry.* But I don't say any of it. Guilt is gnawing at me as we pull up to my house.

"See you at school on Monday," I say, and the words feel all wrong, but I push them out.

I will not tell anyone else about the tumor. I *am* going to be fine. Keeping a secret isn't that big of a deal.

Even though it feels like it is.

14

IT'S WEDNESDAY—MY surgery is two days away—and right now I'm trying to remain calm, but I can't help but fidget in my seat. I'm not nervous about my surgery, but I am nervous about math today. The only positive about everything is that Mrs. Adams agreed to help, so hopefully everything goes according to plan.

Grace smiles at me as she slides into her seat, and Tucker waves at me. I wave back, but turn to face forward because I don't want him to see it on my face. I don't want to give anything away, and I'm afraid he'll take one look at me and know that I'm about to accept his invitation to the dance.

We haven't talked any more about what role his dad played in getting him on tour, but on Monday it was publicly announced that Tucker would be opening for Peyton Matthews on a lot of the big websites and wherever else they announce tour information, so the whole school knows about it. The whole school is *talking* about it. Tucker fell into his role of superstar a little too easily, at least in front of everyone. He acts like he's loving all the attention, because that's what the kids at school seem to expect. His one love is the music, though, so all of the popularity doesn't matter.

It's weird having to share him with everyone, though. People I've never even seen before have started talking to him—and to me by extension, since we've been spending every second we can together—just because he could make it big and *maybe* be really famous someday. Apparently, a lot of people want to be your best friend when that's about to happen. At least, when it's in the music industry or something else equally as exciting.

I'm jittery as Mrs. Adams starts her lesson. I shift in my seat, because even though this was all my plan, I don't actually know when it will happen. I gave her various instructions, but also told her that she could wing it.

Mrs. Adams flips on her projector and I know it's time to take notes for the day. It's how she teaches; she writes out the problems and notes that we copy as she goes through the lesson. It's pretty old-school. Today though, I'm grateful.

We're on our trigonometry unit, which is something I really don't understand. I try to focus on what she's saying, but I can't.

Grace keeps grinning and I glance back at Tucker, but he's focused on taking notes. He has no idea what's about to happen.

I'm sweating when there's only ten minutes left in class. Did Mrs. Adams forget? I talked to her right before class and I know we're on the home stretch of our lesson, because we're doing a homework problem. We solve the problem together and then she writes and says, "Rosie says yes to the dance!"

A few people cheer and look to me, then Tucker. My face is warm from everyone looking at me and I glance back at him; his grin makes me feel warm for completely different reasons.

"This is the greatest class," Kelsey, the only sophomore in the class, says from the front row. She's not wrong though; it's partly the class, but I'm also grateful that Mrs. Adams lets us get away with things that some teachers wouldn't.

"That was great," Tucker says, laughing. "Well done, Rosie, I was totally surprised." Which is exactly what I was going for. Now, if I can only keep my surgery and my tumor a secret for the rest of forever, that would be great.

Tucker wraps his arms around me as we step into the hallway after class. "That was perfect, darlin'." His breath is warm against my ear and I wrap my arms around him, tightening our hug.

I grin. "I wanted it to be a surprise, and something no one ever does. Like who would have their teacher help them answer to a dance? Me, I guess."

His eyes gleam as he hugs me tightly. There are three little words on the tip of my tongue, but they terrify me. I can't say them yet; it's far too soon. We may have known each other for a while, but I don't want to rush our relationship. We've still got time, but I do wonder if he feels the same way about me that I feel about him.

The all-encompassing love that I don't want to fight anymore. If Mom knew, she'd for sure tell me that it's just teenage love and I need to not let myself get swept away. But what if I want to be swept away? What if, for once in my life, I don't want to listen to her practical advice?

I stand up on my toes and press a quick kiss against his lips, smiling at the shocked look on his face as I pull away.

"I thought you weren't into such public displays of affection," he says, grabbing my hand as we head down the hall. Math is our last class of the day, and the hall is nearly empty already since everyone seems to scatter as soon as the last bell rings.

"I'm not," I say. "Or maybe I am, actually. I don't know." I do a weird little skip, but I can't seem to hold in this joy I feel inside.

"Well, whatever is happening right now, I like this version of you, Rosie. It's carefree." He squeezes my hand three times. "And does this mean I can kiss you in the hallway when I want to?"

I squeeze his hand back. Three times for those three little words I'm not quite ready to say out loud. "Maybe." I smirk.

He groans. "You can't tease me like that."

"Why not? It's fun."

He shakes his head. "I think you're going to be the death of me, or at the very least, break my heart into a million pieces."

I stop walking and face him. "Or...we could just never break up and then we'll be each other's forever, and I won't break your heart."

I close my eyes as he leans down and presses a gentle kiss against my forehead. "I like the sound of that, darlin'."

My heart beats erratically in my chest. Maybe we don't have to say those three little words to know how we feel. Maybe that can come later, and for now, I can just enjoy every second of forever that we get.

15

"WHAT'S HAPPENING?" Grace asks over speakerphone. I'm alone for the first time today and in my hospital room. I told my family to go get some food from the cafeteria because even though I can't eat, Mom was getting crabby. I'll be getting prepped for my surgery in a few minutes, so I don't have a ton of time.

But I came up with the perfect excuse for Grace and Tucker, without having to tell them about the tumor.

"Just an emergency surgery," I say into the phone. "My stomach was hurting earlier so we came in, and it's my appendix." The words don't sound forced or rehearsed, and I hope they don't sound like a lie.

"But you're going to be okay?" Tucker asks and my stomach clenches at the worry in his voice. It hurts more every passing day to lie to him, but no one can find out. I could lose my spot at the Paris Ballet Academy, if they are even going to give it to me. But I won't risk it. I don't want anyone to know that I have a tumor.

"I'm going to be totally fine," I say. "I promise."

"And you'll call us as soon as you're done and awake?" Grace asks.

"I'll call as soon as I'm awake and not groggy anymore. Nathan already promised to send you both updates. But this surgery happens all the time, the doctor says it's going to be fine." This part—well, most of it—is actually true. From the scans, Doctor Barker said that as of right now, the tumor doesn't seem to be attached to any major organs, it's just growing in there and it should be an easy removal; then, I'll be cancer-free again.

"Okay," he says, unconvinced. Why did I think I could lie to him? But it's too late now.

"I'm fine, I promise," I repeat. "Okay, well I'm in a little pain, but that's better now that they gave me some meds, and I am going to be fine. It's all going to be fine." I might throw up because of all this lying, but that will be worth it when I make it into the Paris Academy and all of this is behind me. Maybe someday I'll sit Tucker down and tell him the truth, but for now, this is easier for everyone.

There's a knock on my door and I'm surprised to see Lucy standing there. I hold up a finger. "The doctor is back," I say, the lie slipping easily from my mouth. "I'll talk to you later."

"We love you," Grace says.

Tucker adds, "We'll be thinking about you."

"Love you both," I say and then press end.

Lucy enters the room. She's wearing a hospital gown that has purple flowers all over it.

"Your gown is nicer than mine," I say, glancing down at the blue hospital-issued gown I have to wear until I can go home.

"Perks of living at the hospital full-time," she says cheerily. "Anyway, I remembered that you had your surgery today, and I finally got it out of my nurse which room you were staying in, so I wanted to come say hi."

"Hi," I say, setting my phone on the bed next to me and feeling a little awkward.

"Hi," she says, looking around my room. "I'll have my nurse bring over some pictures my little sister has drawn. My walls are really covered, but yours could use some brightening."

"Uh, thanks," I say. I've had only one other group therapy meeting—when I mentioned that my surgery was today—but other than that, Lucy and I didn't talk much last session. She sits on the edge of my bed.

"Are you feeling nervous?"

My heart feels like it's beating in my throat. I've been pretending with everyone else that I'm completely fine about my surgery and everything that's about to happen today. But I really am terrified that something will go wrong and that I won't be able to dance again.

I nod.

She reaches for my hand and I let her take it, even though it's slightly pulling on my IV which is uncomfortable, but I don't let go. "I promise it'll be okay. From what you said, the surgery should be quick and easy and over soon. Plus, I'd think that recovery will be much easier than brain surgery."

I smile at this, because she's probably right.

"I really wish I didn't have to wait a whole month before I can dance again," I complain. As soon as the words are out of my mouth, I regret them. Lucy *lives* in the hospital for months on end, and I'll only miss one month of dance. I can do that. But Lucy doesn't seem bothered by my comment.

"It'll go fast," she assures me.

"I do get to go to the Valentine's Dance with my boyfriend," I say and her eyebrows shoot up.

"Wait, with Tucker, right? That's the boy who kissed you?"

I nod, happy that she remembered.

"It's next week, so I'll still have to take it easy, but he knows I'm having surgery today."

"So you told him?" Lucy asks.

I glance away, my face going warm. I look down at my hands. "Not exactly. I told him and my best friend this morning that I was having some stomach pain and that I have to get my appendix out."

"Won't they know that's not true when there's not a scar on your stomach?" Lucy asks. There's no judgement in her voice, just an honest question.

"I wasn't planning on showing them my scar, even if I had an appendix surgery. I'm not really that kind of person..." I trail off.

Lucy nods. "I get it," she says. There's a moment of silence, then, "I mean, the not telling them part. I do think you should tell them, but I understand why you want to keep it to yourself."

"You'd be the only one," I mumble.

She nods again. "It's like everyone else who does know just wants the world to know, so they don't have to be the only ones watching you, waiting for you to break."

"Exactly." I sit up a little straighter. "I don't want to be the girl with cancer again, I just want to dance and enjoy my life."

Lucy looks sad for a moment, so I rush to add, "Not that being the girl with cancer is a bad thing."

"I knew what you meant," she says, and her smile comes back. "It is hard, when you just want to go on living a normal life. It's easier to pretend when not as many people know."

"Right," I say, and the door to my room opens again. My parents and Nathan enter the room.

"Hi." Lucy waves at them and wastes no time introducing herself. "I'm a friend of Rosie's and just wanted to wish her luck before her surgery." My parents and Nathan look at Lucy, then at me, the question, *You made a friend?* on all of their faces. I roll my eyes. Do they really think I don't know how to make friends?

"We met at group therapy," I say. Dad grins and shakes Lucy's hand. Mom gives her a tight hug and looks like she might cry. Nathan simply eyes me curiously. I haven't told him about Lucy.

"Well, I'll let you all have some time together." Lucy starts toward the door. "I'll come visit once you're done?" she asks and I nod; she's not a bad friend to keep around. In fact, I think I really like her. But I do wish I knew why she was so happy all the time.

"I'll see you later, or tomorrow, whenever I can fully wake up from the anesthesia," I say, and Lucy laughs before heading out the door and back to her own room.

"She seems nice," Dad says, taking Lucy's spot at the edge of the bed and rubbing my foot through the blanket.

"She really is," I tell him. "And somehow more optimistically hopeful than Grace."

Nathan barks out a laugh. "Is that even possible?" He sits on one of the hard chairs in the room, pulling out his phone.

"I didn't think anyone could love life more than Grace, but then I met Lucy." Just then, Doctor Barker comes into the room with another doctor.

"This is Doctor Lisben, she'll be assisting me today and is here to get you prepped for surgery." Doctor Barker turns to my parents. "You're welcome to wait in here or in the waiting area. We'll be taking Rosie now and be done in a few hours."

Mom nods and Dad moves to give me a hug. Nathan also hugs me tightly and says, "I'm praying for you."

I hug him a little tighter. If this were reversed, I would be in hysterics if he were getting rolled back to surgery, but he's surprisingly calm.

I force myself to smile at Nathan as he pulls away. I will be brave. I will not cry. This is going to be simple, and once I wake up, all of this will be over and I can go back to my normal life.

16

I'M groggy when I wake up. But there's light trying to sneak in through the closed blinds. It must be early morning. Nathan is asleep on the small chair in the corner of the room, and Dad's asleep on the cot the nurse must have brought in. I wince as I reach for my phone on the table next to me; the right side of my body is tender.

My phone lights up before I can reach it. Even though it's dark in my room, I see that it's nine in the morning. I must have slept all night after the surgery yesterday, which Doctor Barker said would probably happen. The time also explains why Mom is gone; she's probably at the studio since she has to be there early on Saturdays.

"Hey." I barely get the word out, but my throat is so dry and screaming for water, so I need someone to wake up. Thankfully, Dad wakes up at the sound of my quiet whisper and is by my bedside in an instant.

"Hey, Rosebud," he says, brushing my hair off my forehead. "How are you feeling?"

"Water," I rasp and he grabs the huge mug from the table and holds the straw up to my mouth. Sweet relief.

"You feeling okay?" he asks.

I nod. "Sore, but okay."

He gives my shoulder a squeeze.

Nathan sits up, as if jarred awake by some loud noise. "Dang, I fell asleep again."

Dad laughs. "That's what happens in a dark room, and when you didn't sleep much the night before. I'll go let the nurse's station know you're awake. Doctor Barker will want to come in and talk with us."

"Where's Mom?" I ask, grateful my voice is back to normal and my throat no longer feels like it's going to explode.

"Studio," Dad says, his voice tight. I wonder if they argued about it. They always seemed to argue about her going to the studio when I was going through treatment as a kid. She spent more time at the studio than she did with me at the hospital. It was Dad who was always by my bedside. But Dad doesn't say anything else before he walks out of the room.

"When did Mom leave?" I ask Nathan, who stands up to stretch.

"I think around six this morning." He gives a little shrug. "I can't really remember. She was insistent about not missing a day at the studio. She even yelled at Dad out in the hallway and one of the nurses had to calm her down."

"Wow," I say, even though I'm not that surprised. Nothing would keep her from the studio, not even her daughter having cancer. It's why Dad was with me night and day the last time. It's not that she doesn't care; somewhere deep down I know—or think and hope—that she does, but dance has always been number one in her life, and it probably always will be.

"Any word yet from Doctor Barker?" I ask Nathan.

"Said they got the whole tumor out, you should be good." If I hadn't just had surgery on my side, I might throw my arms up and cheer. Instead, I settle for a modified version of the gesture.

"Woohoo," I say, just as Dad returns with Doctor Barker.

"I see your brother told you the good news." She smiles. "We were able to remove the tumor without any trouble. We'll do some more blood work and another scan before you leave, but I'm confident that we're going to see the results we want. We may still do a round of chemo just to make sure all the cancer is gone, but we'll wait for the blood work to get back before we make any plans."

"That's great," I tell her. While chemo is pretty much the worst thing ever invented, I know it will help. That's what helped the most last time.

Doctor Barker continues, "Whether or not we do chemo, we'll have you come back in another month to run some more tests, make sure things are looking okay. We'll do that every month for the next year, just to keep an eye on everything." What she doesn't say is that they want to keep an eye on me, see if they can figure out why after almost nine years of remission, I grew another tumor. It's not uncommon for cancer to return, but it has been a long time for me. I didn't expect it to come back.

"Okay," I pause. But I have to know, so I ask, "And what happens when I go to Paris in the fall?"

"We'll get you all set up with a doctor over there." Doctor Barker beams at me. She really seems thrilled about how everything went. "It won't be a problem."

I nod in relief. That's good; this won't change any of my plans.

"When do I get to go home?" I ask, and Dad laughs.

"You did just have surgery, but if everything looks good you'll be able to go home tomorrow or the next day, as long as your vitals continue to look good. And I still want you to continue group therapy, at least a couple more times."

"Awesome, I can do that," I say as she turns to leave. "And thank you." She nods before heading out of the room.

"I'm tumor-free!" I say. My stomach rumbles loudly. "And I think I need some food."

"I'll go get us something," Nathan says, leaving the room.

"How are you doing, kiddo?" Dad asks, sitting on the edge of my bed.

"I'm good," I say honestly. I feel a lot less groggy than I expected to after surgery. "How are you?"

"Oh, just getting better all the time, especially now that my girl is okay." He smiles at me. "Mom was thrilled the surgery went well, but she had to get back to the studio."

"I know," I say, without bitterness in my voice.

I'm sorry," he says quietly.

"For what?" I ask. We both know Mom well enough to know this really isn't out of character for her.

"For a lot of things." I raise an eyebrow at him in question, but he doesn't look at me as he continues. "I've always known how she was about ballet. I swore I wouldn't let the same thing happen to you."

"It's not," I say, but the words don't feel quite right in my heart. Am I turning into my mom? Surely not. I'm dating Tucker now, even if my parents don't know about that. I'm doing that for myself. My life isn't only about ballet.

"It is happening." Dad looks at me intently. I don't know when I've ever seen him be so serious. "I thought things would help when you had a different coach, one that wasn't Mom. But you just started dancing more."

"I had to," I try to explain. Doesn't he understand that I didn't do any of this because of Mom, but because of *my* dream to be a professional dancer? "I had to work hard so I could get into the Paris Ballet Academy."

He looks sad. "I just don't want you to throw away the people in your life so you can get to where you want to go in the ballet world."

Anger bubbles in my chest. "I'm not. I won't. You don't think I'm really that much like her?" I don't know what it's like for most little girls, but I've known for a long time that I didn't want to end up like my mother, who was always obsessed with being the best and having her dancers be the best. I mean, I would like to be the best. I sink lower into the pillows, realization washing over me. "Oh gosh, I am just like her."

He comes over to me then and grabs my hand. "No, Rosie, I don't think you are. But you could get there if you're not careful. I think this Tucker boy is the best choice you've made in a long time." I look up at him in surprise. Aren't dads supposed to not want their daughters to get serious with boys when they are teenagers? "I mean, I know you tried to not date him by dating Shawn, which was really dumb by the way, and I know it wasn't real. But I think Tucker is good for you."

"Um, thanks. I think," I say, even though I'm not exactly sure *what* to say to that. I want to tell him that he doesn't need to worry. But maybe dating Tucker isn't enough; maybe I need to do something more than simply date someone to prove that ballet isn't the only thing in my life that I care about.

"Just remember there's more to life than ballet." Dad pats my knee.

I nod as my phone rings, and my heart begins to race as I see the number on the screen.

"It's them," I say, and Dad nods in understanding. The people from Paris are calling.

"Hello." I hope I don't sound nervous. This call could change everything.

"Hello, Rosie," says one of the women who sat on the panel at my audition. "I'm calling to inform you that you have a spot at the Paris Ballet Academy starting in the fall if you choose to accept."

"Yes, yes," I squeal and the woman laughs. "I will be there."

"Wonderful, we're so excited to have you," she says and then we both hang up. Thirty seconds and everything is different. Thirty seconds and the future I've worked for and dreamed about is going to become a reality.

"I got in, Dad!" I exclaim.

He gives my knee another squeeze before sitting back down on the cot. He's smiling, but I can still see concern etched on his face from the conversation we just had.

"I got in. I'm going to Paris!" I sink into the pillows again, this time daydreaming of days full of music and dancing and spending my nights walking the streets of Paris. All is right again; the tumor is out, I'm going to Paris, and I have the best boyfriend and best friends a girl could ask for. Life is good, no—life is perfect.

17

DAD IS GOING over my release papers with a nurse when another nurse pushes Lucy into the room. Lucy, who's in a wheelchair and looks a lot worse than just a few days ago. She's pale and her eyes are bloodshot.

"Sorry I didn't come to see you sooner," she says. Her voice is still so full of life, even though her body is not.

"Oh, no worries," I say, because I can see how exhausted she is. If I were her, I probably wouldn't have come to see me, even if I said I would.

Lucy looks at me like she wouldn't have missed this for the world. "How did it go?"

"All clear," I tell her and I can't help but smile at the words. All clear. Of course, they will still be watching me closely, but I'm one step closer to Paris and back to my normal life.

Lucy grins, a smile that fills her whole face. "Rosie, that's amazing!"

I can tell she'd like to hug me, but her nurse says, "You have to sit." As if she's a dog and not a person. I'm surprised when Lucy listens to her. In the short time I've known her, she seems like the kind of person who does what she wants.

"I'm so happy for you," she says, moving her hand to mine. "I've got an emergency surgery tonight, but I wanted to check in before they prepped me, since my nurse said you're leaving."

"Wait," I say, worry hitting my square in the chest. "Will you be okay?"

Lucy and the nurse both nod. "Yeah, I should be fine. My tumor is just pressing a little too hard against my spine so they're going to go in and remove part of it to help with the pressure."

"But they can't take it all?" I ask.

Lucy shakes her head, and my heart drops into my stomach. She's never going to get the type of news I just got; she might not even get to leave the hospital anytime soon. I was basically just gloating about my good news, and she's about to have another surgery and even more time in the hospital.

"Hey," Lucy says, as if reading my mind. "None of that. I'm going to be fine." Her smile assures me that she will, in fact, be fine. But I don't know how.

"How?" The word slips out and I can feel my dad's eyes on me. I don't know when he came back from signing the release papers, but I know he's watching and listening. "How can you be okay with it?"

Lucy shakes her head. "That is a conversation for another day. I'll see you in therapy next week, or the week after if I'm not able to go," she says brightly.

I guess I'm not getting any answers today. "Of course, I'll see you then." Lucy smiles at me and gives a little nod to her nurse, who wheels her back out of the room. Even though I have the all clear, Doctor Barker thinks it is a good idea for me to continue with group therapy for a while.

"She's a little ray of sunshine, that one," my nurse says and I jump. I'd forgotten she was even in the room. "She's fighting a fight that not many people would, and she does it so well."

My face scrunches up like it does when I'm about to cry, but I'm not sure why I'm feeling all of these emotions. Lucy is a new friend, but I still don't know her that well, and yet my heart goes out to her and what she's fighting. I don't think I'd be able to do it.

"Should we get you out of here?" Dad asks when the nurse leaves with my signed papers. I have to take it easy, but they expect a full recovery.

"Let's go home," I tell him before the nurse comes back to help me out of my hospital gown and into my pajamas.

At home, my bed is comfortable and inviting, and I'm still a little groggy from all of the medication that has been flowing through my body since surgery.

When I open my eyes, I know I've been asleep for several hours. It's dark out now, and Grace is sitting on the floor, painting her nails and talking to Nathan. I blink a few times before realizing that Tucker's arms are around me, my head on his chest.

I'm comfortable for about half a second, before I notice the pain on my right side—where my incision is—and let out a low groan.

"Hey, sleepyhead." He presses a quick kiss on my forehead before gently untangling himself from me. "I'll let your dad know you're awake. I think it's time for more medicine." I nod, not trusting myself to speak. My body hurts.

Dad comes in and hands me water and a pill to take. I sit up a little more, feeling more alert; still in pain, but lighter somehow. The tumor is gone.

"How are you feeling?" Grace asks.

"Great," I say, then laugh. "Okay, well maybe not great. I'm a little sore, but feeling better than I was." Nathan's eyes meet mine at the lie. I was feeling perfectly fine before the surgery; what I'm feeling now is definitely worse.

"Good to hear." She smiles. "Will you be able to go to the dance next week?"

Dad responds before I can. "Her doctor said she could go, but no jumping up and down and she has to take it easy."

"I'll make sure she takes it easy, sir," Tucker says, as if he's a new guy trying to impress my dad. My dad just smiles at him; I think he was impressed with Tucker a long time ago. Remembering our conversation at the hospital makes me wonder how much Dad knows, or guesses, about our relationship.

"I know you will, son," Dad says with a nod before heading out of my room.

"I got into the Paris Academy," I announce, drawing away any attention from my surgery. I don't want any more questions and I really hope they don't ask to see my scar.

"What?!" Grace squeals. "Why didn't you say anything?"

"Um, well, I just woke up and hadn't seen you before that?" It's more of a question than anything, but Grace looks like I've told her she's won a free year at Disneyland.

"That's amazing, Rosie," Tucker says, looking reserved. I turn to him. He's smiling, but it doesn't quite meet his eyes. Isn't he happy for me? This is the one thing I've always wanted, the one thing I've been talking about in all the time I've known him.

"Thanks," I say, instead of asking him what's going on inside his head. "I know I can't really dance for the next few weeks while I heal, but I'll be able to practice again before I know it."

"That's so exciting," Grace says. "Oh, maybe I'll apply to Disneyland Paris so we can hang out and eat all the yummy French food."

"That would be so fun," I tell her honestly, then turn back to Tucker. "And you'll come visit, once the tour is over, right?"

"Of course," he says, sitting on the bed beside me. "I wouldn't miss it for the world." He squeezes my hand three times as I lie my head back against the pillow and watch his face in the dim room.

My heart is bursting. Everything is working out the way it's supposed to.

18

THE THEME for this year's Valentine's Dance is "Black and White Ball." The tickets have strict instructions about what colors we're allowed to wear (black, white, and red) and how if we wear anything else, we'll be turned away at the door.

My dress is black and goes to my knees. There's a band just above my waist and a bow on my right side. I've got my favorite red high heels to wear and Tucker will be in all black with a red tie.

I relax onto Grace's mini sofa as Nathan does my makeup. I'm grateful for an excuse to keep my eyes closed, even if only for a few minutes. I'm still tired from my surgery and tonight is going to be a long one, but everyone has promised to keep an eye on me, and I've promised to take it easy.

Yesterday, Doctor Barker checked my scar and said that I was healing nicely, but that didn't mean I could return to all my normal activities, especially other activities. I am grateful she said I could go to the dance.

"Okay, who do you think is going to be crowned in the Rose Court this year?" Grace asks and I open one eye to look at her. Each year, at the Valentine's Dance, six couples are crowned to the Rose Court. They get crowns and flowers, so it's basically just another excuse to crown someone like a prom queen, only this time, we have no say in who gets picked. Teachers and staff randomly (or maybe not so randomly?) pick people who are at the dance. But seeing as we've never been, we're still unsure of how it works.

"Close please," Nathan commands and I snap my eye shut, but not before I see Grace standing in front of the mirror in her shiny white dress. Our dresses are essentially the same, except for the color. She still hasn't told me who she's going to the dance with though.

"It's definitely going to be Serena. Or maybe Victoria," Nathan says as he uses a brush against my eyelid.

"My vote is Libby," I say. "But it's not like we have a say in it."

"Ooo, she's a worthy contender," Nathan says and I almost laugh. "You are right though, we have no say, but it is always the popular people who get picked."

Grace is friends with a lot of the popular crowd, but she's not exactly in it. She doesn't mind though, because she has always been her own person, ready and willing to do her own thing. I always had ballet and was completely fine with my circle of friends including Nathan, Garce, and eventually Tucker. Nathan might care about all of this more than we do, but only because Emmett could also be picked for the court. They may have broken up, but there's no way Nathan's over him yet.

"I would vote for Libby," Grace says. "She's nicer than Serena and Victoria."

"That's true," Nathan and I say at the same time.

"But she's dating Shawn, are you okay with that?" Grace asks with a strange lilt in her voice. We never really talked about my breakup with Shawn, because it was over so abruptly and then I was with Tucker almost immediately after.

"Why would you even ask that?" I ask. "I don't care at all."

"Just checking." Grace lifts her shoulder and then looks back to the mirror to finish her makeup.

"Why? I'm dating Tucker." Sometimes her logic and questions and ideas about how you should feel about relationships, even after they've ended, confuse me.

"Done," Nathan tells me, stopping Grace from whatever she was about to say. I open my eyes and look in the mirror in his hands. My makeup is what he would call understated, but it's me. I love looking at all the people, including him, who go all out with their makeup, but when I do that, I just don't feel like myself. I like a little glam and sparkle, but not a ton. He used silver, white, and a light shade of red on my eyes.

I give him a hug. "Thank you!"

"Of course." Nathan squeezes me back and announces it's time for both of us to get dressed.

"There's something you should know," Grace tells me as she hands me my dress bag.

"What?"

She holds up her free hand that is covered in glitter. "The fabric of the dress is glittery, right... well, it... kind of gets everywhere."

"Oh my gosh," I say, but then I just start laughing, because of course our dresses would shed glitter. "Tucker might kill us, but I don't mind."

Her eyes go wide. "Crap, I didn't even think about his truck. I mean, I noticed the glitter when I was making the dress, but I assumed it was just because I was moving the fabric around so much."

"But it just gets everywhere?" I'm still laughing.

"It just gets everywhere," Nathan confirms, careful not to touch any part of Grace's dress as he moves around us to grab his own tux. "I'm getting dressed downstairs. I love glitter, but not on me tonight."

Grace starts to say something, but Nathan shoots her a glance and I look back and forth between them, trying to figure out what I'm missing.

"I'm gonna get ready," he says, and then he's out the door.

Grace and I come down the stairs together, possibly leaving a trail of glitter behind. Mom cries as she takes our pictures and Tucker waits patiently for our moms to stop dotting on us.

"You look amazing," he whispers in my ear as we smile for another picture.

"Thank you," I whisper back. "You do, too. You also might be covered in glitter by the end of this." I show him my hands. The glitter seems to be sticking to my arms and fingers more than anything else, but it's also all over Grace's bed where I sat down to put my shoes on.

"Oh boy," he grimaces.

"It wouldn't be a Grace Yang creation without something like this," I say and we both smile.

Mom and Erin both take more pictures, telling us that the ones they take at the dance are always so forced and awkward, and at home they're more relaxed. We even head out to the backyard and get some with the ocean behind us, just before the sun sinks too low, making us all shadows in the pictures.

Then, when we're about ready to leave, Grace and Nathan start taking pictures together. Like a couple.

"What's happening right now?" I ask. Maybe they just didn't want to deal with finding another date, so they decided to go together?

Grace blushes as she looks up at Nathan, and he gives her a hand a squeeze. They stare at each other for a moment before Nathan looks at me. "We're dating."

"But," I sputter...he's gay, isn't he?

He must see my wheels spinning. "Bi, actually." Nathan clears his throat. "Not that I really love labels."

"Right, no, sorry," I stammer. "You've just only dated guys. Well, one guy, Emmett. I thought..." I swallow back the hurt as I trail off; my own twin didn't even tell me he was dating my best friend. And she didn't say anything, either.

Mom and Erin move out of the room, like this isn't news to them. I face Tucker. "Did you know?" I whisper.

He gives me the tiniest of nods. "Not that they're dating. I knew they were going to the dance together."

Well, I guess I wasn't the only one completely out of the loop.

I hug Grace. "You should have told me."

She hugs me back, tightly. "Sometimes, it's just easier to keep secrets."

I catch Nathan's eye over her shoulder and he shakes his head. I hope that means he hasn't told her my secret. While dating my brother and having cancer are two completely different things, I still wish she would have told me.

"I get that," I say instead. I should tell them the truth.

"Should we go?" Tucker asks, ending the moment.

I hold out my hand and give him my best grin, and he gives me one, too.

It's time to go.

Tucker helps me into his truck, which feels surprisingly tall now that I'm in a long dress and heels I know I'll regret later. Grace and Nathan follow behind in Nathan's car.

We stop at a food truck and get some street tacos. It's almost time for the dance, but this is how we planned it. A quick dinner so we could enjoy the dance as much as possible, since none of us really know how long I'll last. I know it's something we're all thinking about, but I'm thankful that Tucker and my friends are pretending that everything is normal and that I didn't just have surgery last week.

I'm eating street tacos at a little table in front of the food truck, napkins spread out over my dress. It all feels so normal. It feels good to be normal. I really want to corner Nathan and ask him when he and Grace started dating, when he realized he was bi. If that's something new or if he's always been attracted to girls, too.

"What are you so smiley about?" Grace bumps Tucker's shoulder, bringing my thoughts back to the table. He's got a soft grin on his face.

"I just get to spend the night with my girl." He winks at me as he says it and I know my cheeks go a little pink. "Why wouldn't I be smiling?" He asks and I smile back at him.

"You are pathetic," Grace laughs and when we stand to leave, the right side of his shirt is completely covered in glitter.

"These dang dresses." He tries to brush some of the glitter from his shirt, but he only seems to be spreading it.

"I swear I didn't realize they were going to be like this. So much glitter came off while I was making them, it's a wonder that there's any left on them at all." Grace gives an apologetic look.

"Well, there is, and it's all over me," he says, but he still reaches for my hand and pulls me in closer.

"Glitter never stops spreading. There's always more than you think," I say, resting my head on his shoulder. Tucker tugs on my hand.

"Glitter is weird," he replies. "Let's get you to the dance."

19

THE VALENTINE'S DANCE is held in the school gym, which usually smells like sweat, but my breath catches when we walk through the doors. It smells clean, and the decorations are stunning.

"You wouldn't even know that just yesterday people were playing basketball in here," Grace says, the awe in her voice matching what I feel.

The parent volunteers who decorate really went all out this year. There are several round tables surrounding the open dance floor, covered with silver tablecloths, and there are red paper hearts everywhere. In the middle of the dance floor, a disco ball shines down, reflecting the splashes of silver throughout the room. Nearly every wall is covered with black and white cloth hanging from the ceiling.

"Are you sure we're not in a tent?" I ask, only half-joking.

"It's still the gym," Tucker says, pointing above us. "There's the basketball hoop." The rest of us look up, but even the hoop has been covered with the same billowing fabric that covers the walls.

"Well, I can see why people love this dance," I say. I'm still sore and a little weak from my surgery, but I won't let that ruin my night. Everything looks amazing, and I'm here with Tucker. I couldn't ask for anything better.

We spend the next couple of hours dancing. Tucker always seems to have an arm around me, holding me close, even during the fast songs. Not that I can really dance to those anyway.

"This is perfect," I whisper to him as another slow song starts. He smiles and presses a kiss against my forehead.

When a new song starts playing, I move away from Tucker, eyes widening as I take him in.

"Oh my gosh." There is glitter on every part of his suit.

"I don't even want to look." He groans and his eyes don't leave my face, but I can't look away from his black jacket, which is covered in glitter. As are our hands, faces, hair, and basically anything we've touched. The glitter has definitely multiplied, because my dress looks exactly the same as it did when I put it on.

"That's probably a good idea," I say as he starts jumping to the beat. I give a little bounce, but wince in pain.

"Water break?" he asks, and I nod. We make our way to the table covered with cookies, punch, and water. He grabs both of us a cup of water and leads me to the chairs that line the wall.

We're not the only ones sitting out. The dance has been going for two hours now, and I'm glad I'm not the only one who's feeling tired. I'm actually feeling better than I expected—a tiny miracle.

"So, has this been the dance of your dreams?" he asks.

"I don't know if I ever really dreamed about dances like this, not in the same way that Grace did. But she is the one who loves all the princess movies." I give his hand three squeezes. "It has been perfect, though."

"I'm glad." He squeezes my hand back when Missy and Amber appear in front of us.

"You shouldn't be with her," Missy says, jerking her head toward me. Tucker's fingers tighten around mine. "You should still be with Amber. Or even me, but I don't like you. Amber does, though." Our heads all swing to Amber, who's bright pink.

Tucker coughs. "Um."

"She's just a selfish brat, you should be with someone who isn't so self-obsessed," Missy says loudly, and several people look in our direction. It's clear the punch was spiked and she's had a little too much to drink, judging by the way she sways on her feet—but her words still sting. I'm not self-obsessed—she doesn't even know me, how could she say that?

"Let's go, Missy." Amber tugs at her arm, but Missy ignores her.

"You deserve to be with a girl who cares about someone other than herself," Missy says as Amber pulls her away and mouths, 'I'm sorry,' to us. But the damage is done.

He deserves to be with someone who isn't selfish.

He deserves to be with someone who isn't self-obsessed.

He deserves to be with someone who isn't a liar.

The words bounce around in my head, the last one making me freeze. Missy didn't say that, but I am a liar. I've been pretending everything is fine and not telling him the truth when I should have. I glance at Tucker. He deserves someone better than me.

"No," he starts, knowing exactly what's going on in my head. "Rosie, no."

"You do," I whisper, as if saying the words quietly will stop the flood of emotions that's pouring through my body.

"I only want you," he whispers back. I can see the sincerity in his eyes. I feel it in his voice and with his hand in mine.

He deserves to be with someone who isn't me.

I choke out a sob, feeling strangely emotional; normally what girls at school say about me doesn't get to me, but tonight, it does. He pulls me to my feet, leading me through the ballroom, away from everyone who seems to be watching us and out into the cool air. We end up sitting in his truck. I don't look at myself in the mirror, but I'm sure my mascara has been cried off or is streaking down my face.

"Rosie," he starts but I just shake my head. Nothing he could say will change anything. Have I been selfish, to keep him for myself? To love him and keep him close even though it's going to kill him when I've gone to Paris?

These thoughts bring a fresh set of tears. I can't even look at him. He's holding my hand, a connection I don't want to sever. My phone vibrates. *Good, a distraction,* I think, and pull it out of my bag.

TUCKER

Ordinary by Alex Warren

I look at him as music fills the truck. It's a song I know I've heard before, because it's on our playlist, but I've never really listened to it.

Tucker starts singing along, staring straight at me as he does. My heart breaks into a million pieces, but it's like he starts to pick them up and put them back together as he sings. The emotion in his voice is raw and I wonder if he's going to start crying, but he just keeps looking at me and singing along.

I'm quiet when the song ends and a new one starts.

"I don't want to be with anyone but you," he says quietly. "I know that you love dance and that it'll always be a big part of your life. Sometimes it makes me crazy when all you seem to think about is what you want." His voice catches. "But I want to be with you. And it's not true what she said, because you do care about more than just yourself, and anyone who knows you knows that."

I nod, because I can't seem to find words. I want to believe him, but Missy's words won't stop rattling in my head. Along with my own thoughts. I need to tell him the truth.

"Are you—" I start, but he cuts me off.

"Yes, I'm sure." He takes in a breath. "I love you, Rosie."

"I think I love you, too," I say and he just shakes his head, laughing.

"Seriously, you're going to pull the 'I think' again?"

I start laughing too.

"Okay, okay, I do love you. I think." We both laugh again, a feeling of calm settling over us. "I just don't know how to be sure. I mean, I'm only eighteen. Can you really feel that way about someone at eighteen?"

"Yeah." He sounds so sure. "You can."

"How do you know?" I ask. My heart and head are both pounding. I'm exhausted and his confession feels so right, but it's also making me second-guess everything. I need to tell him about the tumor.

"I know, because it's how I feel about you," he says and squeezes my hand three times. "When I do that, I'm telling you I love you."

"I like that," I say, and it's true, because now we have something that's just ours. A way to say how we feel without having to actually say it. Not that he really needs to say it; I can tell by how he looks at me—and how he treats me—exactly how he feels.

Tell him now. The thought startles me. I know I should tell him about the tumor. Tell him that it wasn't my appendix they took out last week. But even with Missy's outburst, tonight has been so good and I don't want to ruin this moment. I will tell him the truth, just not yet. I don't want to ruin tonight.

Instead, I say, "I love you, and I'm tired."

"Well then, let's get going," he says. I close my eyes on the way home, paying attention to the music and the way his hand feels in mine. I open my eyes when we stop.

"This is your house," I say, stupidly. Maybe he knows I have something else that I need to tell him, and this will be my chance.

He smiles. "Yeah, quick pit stop before I take you home." He hops out of the truck and opens the door for me. "Come on."

"What are we doing?" I ask.

"It's a surprise." He smiles, as if he's got a million more surprises up his sleeve.

He leads me to the backyard, toward Kenny and Micah's clubhouse. It used to be their dad's shed until he converted it into a space for them to be loud and crazy—outside of the house. I shiver in the cool ocean breeze as he pulls me inside.

It looks nothing like it did the last time I saw it, when it was covered with toy trucks and beanbag chairs. Now there's fairy lights all around the floor and a pile of blankets made into a makeshift bed in one corner. His guitar is resting on the ground next to it.

"I thought tonight would be a good night to share an original with you." He leads me to the pile of blankets and we both sit. He runs his hand through his hair, the way he does when he gets nervous.

"I wrote this song right after the Fourth of July last year, when you left for Paris," he says, and I hear the unsaid meaning in his words, when he thought that all of this was going to happen back then. "I was missing you a lot, and at the time, I thought we were going to be together when you got back. Life didn't work out that way, but I'm glad you're mine now. It's not quite finished, but I've got some of the lyrics done."

I smile. We've been able to move on from the past. We're together now. "I don't think anyone has ever written me a song before."

He gives me a shy smile. "This one's for you, darlin'." He winks, and then he closes his eyes and starts to play.

We've been young and reckless
With you standin' in that dress

Everything's been all a mess
But now you're mine

Took forever for us to come 'round
Scared of taking chances, puttin'
Our hearts on the line
But now you're mine

I'm grinning like a fool by the time he's finished. "Wow!"

He ducks his head like he's embarrassed. "Good wow?"

"Great wow!" I scoot over so I can give him a hug once he sets his guitar down. "That was incredible. I need you to do that all the time now. I loved having my own private concert."

He wraps an arm around me. "Who knew it would be this easy to get you to fall in love with me?" From where we're sitting, I can see out the small window, where the full moon is shining bright.

"Nah, I don't know if this would have worked. I had to fall in love with you first. I just didn't realize that's what I was feeling."

"Still, I should've just sang for you," he says, pulling me closer. I feel his lips press against my hair and I let out a sigh.

"Why do you think I made that rule in the first place?" I tease.

"You're the worst."

"But I'm yours now, or maybe you're mine, so it all worked out, right?"

"It all worked out," he says, and I'm hoping he'll kiss me, but instead he pushes himself off the ground, holds out his hand to me, and helps me up. "Now let's get you home and back in bed to rest."

I stand on my toes and give him a quick kiss, my heart thundering in my chest. "I have one more thing I need to tell you." My voice is barely more than a whisper.

Concern flits across his face.

"It wasn't my appendix, it was a tumor," I whisper. "They got it all out. I may have to go back in for more blood work and tests, but the doctor said everything looks good and I might not even have to do chemo."

He stares at me.

"I'm sorry I didn't tell you." I glance down. "I just didn't want to be the sick girl again. You know?"

He nods, slowly. So slowly that I know I've ruined everything.

"You're okay though?" he asks.

"Yes. All clear now." At least, I should be. I know there's a possibility of more growth in the future, but Doctor Barker didn't see any signs of tumors anywhere else on my scan. "I'm good."

"Then that's all that matters." He pulls me into a tight hug. "That doesn't change anything for me, okay?"

I nod against his chest. I really shouldn't have been so afraid to tell him. I need to tell Grace, but I'm not sure I'm ready for that conversation yet. I don't know if she'll be as forgiving.

"I love you," he whispers against my hair, pressing his lips to my head. I close my eyes, relishing this feeling. See, I didn't have to worry. He still loves me.

"I love you, too," I whisper back. A weight that's been on my chest suddenly feels lighter. I told him the truth, and he didn't run away. I didn't ruin anything.

He tugs on my hand. "Let's get you home, or I might spend all night kissing you, and I don't think your mom would appreciate that."

I laugh. "Probably not."

He gives my hand three squeezes, and I do the same.

journal entries from the past two weeks

FEBRUARY *4*

Dear Journal,

Hi, yeah, it's me, Rosie, again. It's been a while since I last wrote in this journal, or even wrote in general. I'm still not sure why I picked up this journal to write in today, since I'm not even writing about Tucker, which is what most of the old entries are about. I mean, we are together now!! But that's not why I'm writing.

I had another tumor.

I was months away from being 9 YEARS in remission and I got a new tumor. One that I didn't even feel or know I had. I just got home from the hospital. I had surgery to have it removed.

I'm still sore and recovering (obviously), but Tucker and Grace finally left and I can finally feel relieved that my tumor is OUT OF MY BODY! See, they don't know. I didn't tell them. I lied the day of the surgery and said it was an emergency surgery to get my appendix out. Now, I do feel sort of bad about that, but things have just been so good with me and Tucker, and even me and Grace, and with dance, and I didn't want to ruin any of it.

So I lied. I feel bad. My appendix is fine, and still in my body.

But I can't seem to find the words to tell them. They don't suspect a thing, which makes it a little easier. I'm just so mad about it and I'm not ready to bring my anger into my new relationship.

I don't think Tucker's noticed yet, because when I'm with him it's easier to pretend that everything is fine. It's easy to pretend that it's just us against the world and that hard things don't happen to us. We don't really talk about the hard stuff, and right now, I'm okay with that.

We hold hands, and he kisses me every chance we get. We don't think about how in the summer, he'll go on tour, right before I leave for Paris.

I think Grace can tell something is up, even though she hasn't actually asked me about it. Nathan told me after they left that I need to say something, that I need to tell them. After all, she's my best friend and Tucker's my boyfriend.

But I'm just so mad about the tumor.

How could my cancer come back after everything I've been through? How could God (if there is a God) do this to me? Why is this happening? Why now, when I found out earlier today that I got into Paris? I know the surgery went great and the tumor is gone, but what if something else is wrong? What if Doctor Barker actually missed something? And maybe she didn't, maybe she's right, but I still have to go in once a month (even in Paris) for scans and tests to make sure I'm still all clear.

I thought my body was past this. I thought I was done with all the pokes and prods and lying still in a huge tube.

I can't dance for at least a month or two. That seems like a lifetime.

I don't know who I am without dance.

I'm scared that my career will be ruined because of this, because I don't have this time to train and work toward Paris. I got in, yes, but I can tell that Mom's worried about me not dancing for a month (or even longer).

I love dance, but I loved it when it was just fun. Right now, it doesn't feel fun. It feels like I've had a limb ripped off my body, like I can't breathe.

None of this seems fair.

And then there's Lucy. This girl I met at cancer therapy. She's so happy and bright and cheery and it makes me insane. She's got this brain tumor and basically just lives from surgery to surgery because there's nothing she can do. She has it worse than I do (so why am I complaining??? I mean, my life still sort of feels like it's over, like something has shifted) but how is she still so happy? How does she still smile and ask me how my day was when she's obviously in so much pain?

Part of me really wants to hate her, but I also kind of like her and I guess there's a part of me that wishes I could be more like her. But then I go back to not liking her because she's dying and seems so happy still. I don't get it.

UGH.

I need to tell them. Maybe I will after the Valentine's Dance next week. Grace already made our dresses and I just want it to be a fun night. I don't want to have to worry about telling them or having them worry about me the whole time.

I just want to enjoy my life, cancer-free.

Even though I'm technically not cancer-free anymore...

Still hoping the biopsies they did on some of the nearby lymph nodes come back negative (I can't ever remember how to spell the word that means they don't have cancer) because then I won't need any further treatment! But I don't know when I'll find out that news.

Love, Rosie

February 14 - The Valentine's Dance

Dear Journal,

Tonight, Tucker told me he loves me!

HE LOVES ME!

I've never had anyone other than family say those words to me, AND I said them back. Wow.

I didn't know that you could feel this way.

In honor of those three little words that make me feel like the luckiest girl in the world, I am going to make a list of some of my favorite memories with Tucker. Grace gave me the idea a while ago when she did the same thing when she was dating Leo. OH. She's dating NATHAN now! Neither of them told me. I'll write about that another time though, tonight is just for memories of us together.

1. The day I met him. That was the first time I wrote in here, so I won't really write about it again, but I am so glad he came into my life.

2. Two years ago, we went to a corn maze/fall festival with several of our friends. Everyone else actually had a date, except me and Tucker, so we were unofficially pushed together into a date we didn't mean to be on. I wasn't feeling great because I was on my period, but Tucker was doing stupid things, trying to make me laugh the whole time. Then, there was one moment when we were alone in the corn maze because everyone had either rushed ahead or the others were behind us, and I swear I thought he was going to kiss me. He was looking at me like he wanted to. Instead, though, we heard Grace yelling from up ahead and ran to catch up to her. That was one of the first times I really wondered what it would be like to kiss Tucker Bensen.

3. One day at lunch, shortly after Tucker had moved here, Grace and I found him sitting on one of the school stairwells. He had his head in his hands and Grace immediately went into what we call her 'mom mode' of trying to figure out what was wrong. I wasn't sure what to do—at that point, we were friends, so it wasn't weird for me to sit on the step by him and put my arm sort of around him and rub his back. My dad did that whenever Nathan or I were upset and it always helped us feel better. Tucker eventually told us that his dad had called him, saying there was no way Tucker would make it big unless he accepted his help. And I guess he also said a lot of other mean things, but we were able to calm Tuck down and assure him that no matter what happened, he was a good singer and that he could still do something in the music world if that's what he wanted.

I'm not sure why that's one of my favorite memories with Tucker, but I feel like we were better friends after that.

4. Last summer, right before the 4th of July, we all went swimming together. Me, Grace, Nathan, and Tucker. It was on one of my rare non-dance days, and I was able to just relax and have fun. While we were inside, waiting to get snacks at the small concessions stand, Tucker jumped up—why, we still don't know. But the ceiling was so low that he hit his head! It was hilarious, and naturally, we teased him about it for months after.

5. Shortly after we met, Tucker and I were hanging out at his house. Grace was in charge of the twins, so she'd gone upstairs to get them a snack, and right now, I can't remember where Nathan was, since he was usually with us. But out of the blue, Tucker says:

"We should be best friends forever."

I think I smiled and said something like, "Yeah, we should." But I remember thinking... can you really be best friends with a guy forever when you're a girl? Will that mean we become something more at some point? I didn't ask any of those questions, but after that, whenever he saw me, he'd say, "Hey, best friend." And just like that, we were best friends, but in a different way than Grace and I have ever been.

Okay, I think that's enough for now. I'm dating Tucker. He loves me. How did I get so lucky?

Love, Rosie

P.S. I told him about the tumor. I also told him that I'm all clear, and good to go. Which, technically, I still don't know that news, but I feel good. Doctor Barker was so optimistic and said there wasn't anything coming up on my original scans, so that I should be in the clear. But I told him. He still loves me. I don't know why I was so scared to tell him about the tumor.

I'm not sure how to tell Grace, though. She didn't tell me about her and Nathan (not that he said anything either) but she's my best friend, and I feel like she'll be mad. So I may wait a little longer to tell her...

20

"TODAY WE'RE GOING to be doing something different," Doctor Simpson, our group therapist, declares. It's followed by a collective groan and I shift anxiously in my seat. Every time I've come to therapy, it's been the same. We go around the circle and she asks each of us various questions, which we can answer if we feel comfortable or pass if we don't want to talk about it.

I'm not sure I like different. Plus, this is probably one of my last sessions since Doctor Barker called yesterday to say that my lymph nodes were benign.

"I'm going to split you up into pairs and you'll be talking with each other today." Doctor Simpson gives us all an encouraging grin. "Obviously, you're not trained therapists, so I'll be moving from group to group if anyone needs extra help. The point of this exercise is to get talking and to listen to your partner. Sometimes, simply talking to someone who's going through something similar to you can be helpful."

My stomach flips. I glance around the group and everyone seems to look as nervous as I feel. This isn't exactly what we signed up for.

"Could I use the bathroom before we get started?" I ask as Doctor Simpson starts putting people in pairs.

"Of course, but hurry back."

I nod, feeling better almost as soon as I'm out of the room. I don't like talking about feelings, especially not with someone I only see every few weeks.

I stand by the bathroom sink for as long as I risk it before heading back; the giant clock at the edge of the room says that I was gone for less than five minutes.

"Great," I mutter under my breath. I'm still going to have to partner up with someone.

"Rosie, you'll be with Lucy today," Doctor Simpson waves me over to where she's sitting with Lucy. The tightness in my chest lessens slightly. I can talk to Lucy.

"Sorry I ran off there," I say lightly. "I don't like things like this."

"It's okay," Lucy says. "There's always a few who run out whenever Doctor Simpson changes things up. I told her I didn't mind waiting for you. I thought you'd be more comfortable since you know me and all. I hope that's okay."

I relax at her words. "Yes, totally okay. Thank you so much."

"I can start if you want," Lucy volunteers.

"That'd be great."

"Okay." She clasps her hands together in her lap, but I know they won't last there—she talks with her hands, and it's one of the things I love about her. There's a lump in my throat at the thought. I'm two weeks post-op, which means she is, too. I can tell she's tired and she came here in a wheelchair, but she's still here. I'm glad she's still here. It's hard to swallow the lump.

"I feel like talking about God today," Lucy says.

I blink at her. "Um, okay." I move my hands so I'm sitting on my fingers. I didn't grow up in a religious home. I know my dad prays sometimes, but it's not something we ever really talk about. I know a lot of people believe in God, but I've never really thought about it.

"I was so mad at Him when I first got cancer," she says, and I nod, because I understand that. I was mad, too, when my new tumor grew. "I didn't understand why this was happening to me, you know? I still have so much of my life ahead of me, why was this happening? Why now?

"I've spent a lot of time yelling at God the past few years. Literally yelling. Maybe He doesn't appreciate that, but sometimes you just gotta yell." She smiles a little, as if she finds this humorous.

I close my eyes, trying to picture Lucy yelling, and I cannot do it. She doesn't seem like a person that would ever yell.

"But then, as more time passed, the yelling stopped, and something changed."

"What changed?" I find myself asking.

"I wasn't so angry anymore."

I meet Lucy's eyes at this—how is she not still angry? If I were her, I think I'd still be angry.

"I woke up one day and I thought, 'Wow, I'm so grateful to be alive. I'm so grateful that I have amazing nurses and doctors. I finally see God's hand in this.' And after that, the anger was just gone."

Now I'm skeptical. "Just like that?" That seems too easy. Like some magical thinking can make everything better.

"Just like that." Lucy smiles. "I mean, I don't think it actually happened just like that. Most things that happen don't just happen, it's usually a long build-up of smaller moments that lead up to that big moment, the one people say changes everything."

I'm still not sure I believe her.

"I realized that even though cancer sucks, and it's really, really hard to have a brain tumor, God is still here. He's still in the details and he's still with me."

"Even though He won't take the cancer away?" From what I

understood, isn't God supposed to perform lots of miracles, including healing the sick?

"Sometimes He doesn't take the hard things away." Lucy says it like it's no big deal, like she's gonna keep trusting God anyway, even though He's essentially letting her suffer.

"But why not?" I ask, suddenly desperate for the answer, when Doctor Simpson calls us back together. How can she believe in something that doesn't make her better?

"I'll tell you later," Lucy says, as we move back into our semi-circle and do a shorter version of our usual therapy session.

I can't focus for the rest of the session. I don't really listen as Don talks about losing his wife to cancer, and how he now has a tumor on his liver. Or when Beth talks about how she's dealing with her diagnosis. I mean, I hear their words, but none of it makes sense. The only thing running through my head is that I need to talk to Lucy as soon as this is done, and she needs to explain.

As soon as our session is over, I can tell that Lucy is in no shape to talk; her eyes are droopy as her nurse starts to push her wheelchair. "We'll talk soon," she promises, as I'm left standing there with a thousand questions burning in my mind.

I'm quiet on the car ride home. How can there be a God when so many bad things are happening in the world? Why doesn't He stop any of it? Why would anyone choose to believe in a being or person or whatever God is, when He doesn't take away the hurt, when there are still starving people in the world, and evil people running the world? Doesn't He care?

He has a weird way of showing it, if He does. I fold my arms over my chest. I will not cry, even though I kind of want to. Even though I already had questions about my own cancer, Lucy's confession today did nothing to soothe them; if anything, it made the gnawing in my chest even worse.

It isn't supposed to be like this. Life isn't supposed to be like this. I'm not as far gone as Grace and Tucker to really believe in a happily ever after for everyone, and I know that bad things happen, but this? I just don't get it. I don't get it at all.

"You okay, Rosebud?" Dad asks quietly, interrupting my spiral.

"I'm fine," I say, because I don't know how to actually say what I'm thinking and feeling.

"You're awfully quiet," he says as we pull off the freeway, but instead of turning left to go home, he turns right, toward the beach. Toward the water. "I know that when I get really quiet, it means there's something on my mind that I probably should talk about, but don't quite know how."

I'm quiet for a moment. First I'm annoyed that I'm so much like him, he knows almost exactly what's happening inside my brain, and then, I'm grateful that he understands me in this small way.

"I just don't get it," I finally say.

We pull into the parking lot by the pier; it's a Thursday afternoon in February, so the lot, and the beach, are nearly empty.

"What don't you get?" Dad asks and I look out at the sparkling water over the hood of the dashboard.

I watch the waves for a long time, and he doesn't push. It's as if he knows I'll talk when I'm ready and he's fine waiting. We can simply watch the ocean together until then.

The waves slow my heart, but don't clear my head. Maybe talking, like Doctor Simpson said earlier, will help.

"I was almost nine years clear," I whisper. "Why this? Why now?" I look at Dad then, and he's watching me, waiting for me to say more. When I open my mouth again, I'm nearly yelling. "Why does Lucy, who is so good and so happy, have that stupid tumor that they'll never be able to fully remove? She's just gonna keep having surgeries until she dies. How is that fair? How is she so freaking happy? How does she still believe in God when He's obviously not helping her?"

Dad lets out a slow breath and looks out at the water.

"I need answers, Dad." My voice cracks in the middle and the tears that were threatening to spill begin to slide down my face.

"I know, bud." He's still looking out at the water. "But sometimes we don't get all the answers."

"Seriously?" I choke on a sob. "That's all you've got for me?" Without thinking, I push open the door and I'm running toward the beach. The frigid water splashes up to my ankles when I finally stop, registering the pain in my right side. Running may not have been the smartest idea so soon after my surgery.

"Rosie." Dad's right next to me, standing in the freezing water. "I don't have all the answers, but I will say this."

I look at him, the wind whipping my hair across my face, but I don't care. What's the point of any of this, if at the end of the day, there's just so much pain and suffering for everyone?

"I know we never really raised you to believe in God, and it was just one of those things where we wanted you to find answers for yourself. But maybe I should have said something more. Do you know why I love the ocean so much?"

I shake my head no, because even though I've heard him talk about the water nearly every day of my life, I get the feeling that what he's about to say is going to be different this time.

"When I stand here and look out at the water, I feel so, so small," he says, and I nod. I feel that way right now; the ocean goes on forever. I'm just a tiny spec against the vast blue in front of me. "But at the same time, I also feel so big and so significant."

I blink. I don't know if I've ever felt that way. "Why?"

"I believe that God made the earth and the ocean, and that He also made you and me," he says, and it's not the first time I'm hearing the words, but it's the first time I'm hearing it from *him* and I'm not sure what that means yet. "He made this beautiful ocean, this huge part of the world that holds so many wonders, so many things that we don't even know about. There's beauty in it, and it just leaves me in awe."

I look at him again as he continues. "And then I look at you, my only little girl, and even though you're eighteen, you're always gonna be my baby girl." He's got tears in his eyes now. "And I look at you, and I think all those same things that I do about the ocean. That there's still so much to know about you, that from the moment we met you, we thought you were perfect, and holding you in my arms that first time, I was in awe. Because here I was, still a fairly new dad who went from no kids to two, and now one of them was a girl and one was a boy, and how was I supposed to raise the two of you? What was I supposed to do?"

His eyes never leave mine. "Yet, I just knew that there was something greater out there, bigger than you and me. That we get to take part in a tiny little bit of the beauty that He created. I'm so grateful."

"But what about the hard stuff?" I ask, my voice quiet.

"Remember when you first got cancer?" I nod—of course I remember. Chemo made me so sick. "I got down on my knees that night and begged God to take it from you, to make you well. I said I'd do anything, give anything to free you from that pain and every-thing you had to go through.

"But that's not how God works." Dad steps closer to me, pulling me into a hug. "It's not how parenting works. You don't want your kids to go through hard things, but sometimes you can't change it, sometimes you can't take away their pain."

"I thought God was supposed to be all powerful or whatever, and could do anything."

"You know, He probably can," Dad says, and I can hear the smile in his voice. "But I imagine that sometimes He doesn't, because maybe we need to go through it. Just like sometimes when a kid crashes on his bike, the parents can't run to him right away, they need to see if he'll get up on his own to prove to himself that he is strong, that he's okay."

I don't want to have to prove that I'm strong.

"But there's just so much bad... so many hard things... it doesn't make sense," I say into his chest.

"Well, I guess that's something you need to think about, and maybe ask Him about," he says, letting go of me.

"I don't exactly know how to pray," I admit. "Or even know if I actually want to."

"Well, just think about it then; you'd be surprised by what happens when you just take some time to think."

I nod. "Can we go now? I think my toes are frozen."

Dad laughs. "Sure kiddo, let's go home."

I follow him back up the beach, toward his car. Pausing only once to look out at the bright blue ocean, and I feel a little lighter. I'm still confused, but maybe we really aren't supposed to have all the answers. That doesn't mean I'll stop thinking about the things that don't make sense to me. Maybe bad things will always still happen, and maybe there isn't always some greater reason for it, maybe it's just the way life is. Maybe someday, I can be okay with that.

journal entries - present day (march - april)

MARCH *1*

Dear Journal,

My tumor is gone—my last blood test came back clear. Which is a great thing, but I still feel so... confused, and so lost.

For the past ten years of my life, my number one goal was to become the best ballerina I could (and possibly the best in the world.) It's all I talked about with Mom, it's all I talked about with anyone. Getting into Paris was the next step in my big dream, because once I got into the dance academy there, I was all set for my future. Dance for several years, tour with some big companies if I wanted to, then retire young.

But now I'm not so sure if that's what I want. Or maybe I'm just feeling guilty that I have these big dreams that are actually falling into place, when my friends aren't having that experience.

Obviously, I'm not talking about Tucker. He'll be famous before anyone; people already know his name.

Yesterday, Grace was over at my house and we were painting our nails. She didn't get into the college she wanted, which means she's going to start at the community college instead because she didn't apply to any backups. She really wants to work at Disneyland, but she isn't sure she'll be able to do that now that her new school will be almost an hour away from the park.

I was/am devastated for her, but almost as soon as she told me about everything that was going on, she said, "But I'll figure it out," and then started telling me (finally) how things with her and Nathan developed.

The way she explains it was that it just kind of happened. That one day they were friends and the next one of them was flirty, and it all kind of snowballed from there.

I didn't ask about Nathan's sexuality; he and I have talked about that a little. Basically, he said that being bisexual fits him the most, since he's attracted to guys and girls. When I asked him how long he's known this, he said basically forever. Even if Grace is the first girl he's ever dated. I'm just glad we were finally able to talk about it.

I've been on quite a few dates with Tucker, and yet... I don't think I've ever told Grace about them. Maybe because most of the time he's with us, so it would feel weird.

But I feel like it's something different. I keep thinking about all the conversations I've had with Grace and Lucy over the past year, and now I'm second-guessing myself. Is dance really not the most important thing in my life? I mean, I still love my family and I really care about Tucker, but dance is what gives me life, so why is everyone (okay, well, not everyone, but it sure feels like it) saying that there are more important things than dance?

I just don't know anymore. How can something I love be the 'wrong thing' to focus on?

Love, Rosie

March 7

    Dear Journal,

Today I had to go to the hospital because my scar from where they cut me open was really hurting, and Doctor Barker just wanted to make sure everything looked okay.

Apparently, this is normal and I'm just a wimp when it comes to pain, which, when she implied that, made me want to laugh, because I dance until my toes are bleeding and I would keep going if it weren't for the people who make me stop. I'd dance forever if I could, even if it made my feet fall off.

Okay. That was kind of a gross image, but really. I'm a wimp when it comes to pain. Doctor Barker didn't actually say that, but that's what it felt like she was saying.

I haven't talked to Dad or Lucy about God anymore, but I am thinking about all the things they said. I still don't have any answers, but I don't feel as mad about it as I did before.

Love, Rosie

March 18

Dear Journal,

I feel like not much is happening. I still haven't been given permission to dance, which is KILLING ME. But I go to the studio every day. I help Mom out with the little girl classes and sometimes I just sit in one of the empty practice rooms and listen to my audition piece, even though my audition is over.

Nathan is upset with me for not telling Grace about my tumor, but he pretends to be fine when we're all together, which I'm grateful for. If we're alone, he rarely talks to me. I miss him, I miss talking to him. We talked about him and her a little and he said the same thing she did, but I feel like he avoids me most of the time. Which I really hate. I just don't know how to tell her. Tucker was so under-standing, but I don't think Grace will be. She doesn't think we have any secrets between us (even if she didn't tell me about her and my brother) and she'll hate me forever if she finds out I didn't tell her about the tumor.

I spent so much time before my audition (and right after it) talking about how I couldn't wait to just be 'normal' and not have anything going on. Turns out, I really don't like it...

Love, Rosie

April 30th

Grace found out.

21

I'M in Grace's kitchen. Erin, Grace's mom, is making dinner, and I'm waiting for Tucker to get home from work—which tonight is singing at the bar during their afternoon happy hour—so we can go on our date.

"Why didn't you go watch him sing?" Grace asks me as she peels a banana, and my stomach rolls. She's barely said a word to me since she found out about my tumor and the real reason I had surgery. She found out two days ago when my mom slipped up and told me something about Lucy. I'm not mad at Mom; I'm glad it's out in the open, but just like I thought, Grace hasn't forgiven me.

"He asked me not to, said he had something special for us planned and didn't want me to be all mushy before the date even started."

Erin smiles at me. "He sure does love you, ya know?"

"I know." I smile at her.

"You need to tell him, Rosie," Erin says, and my gaze cuts to Grace.

"What?" Grace asks. "I had to tell someone."

"I already did," I say.

162

"Really?" Grace hits the counter, making me jump. "Or will you just wait until he accidentally hears your mom talking about it? Because there's no way he's been with you for three months and knows and didn't tell me."

"Grace," I start, but she holds up a hand. She didn't believe that I had already told Tucker when I said that after she found out. She still doesn't believe me, and apparently, Erin doesn't think I did, either. Apparently, they think he should still be mad at me for lying, but he hasn't been mad the entire time. He was just thankful I told him and glad that I'm okay now.

"I don't even want to hear it," she says before walking out of the kitchen.

I look at Erin. "I am sorry. I was just worried about what she'd say and how she'd treat me. I just didn't want it to be real, so I figured that pretending it wasn't would make it easier. But I told him, right after the dance, and he forgave me for lying."

"They care about you sweetheart," Erin says, kneading the dough for cinnamon rolls in front of her. "You should have told her sooner."

"I know," I say. "But I didn't, and I don't know what else to do other than apologize about keeping it from her.

"Just give her time," Erin says. "She just needs time to adjust to the news."

"I know."

"You know what?" Tucker asks, entering the kitchen, and I smile brightly at him, hoping it doesn't look too forced.

"I know that she won't hate me forever for not telling her about the tumor," I say.

He raises an eyebrow at me. "I thought you already told her. I mean, she and I haven't talked about it, but I thought she knew."

I look down, ashamed. "I didn't know how to tell her, so I didn't, and then she found out when my mom said something and now she's mad."

"She'll get over it," he says, grabbing my hand. "You're her best friend, and you're fine now; she can't stay mad forever."

I nod, trying to believe him, but ready to think about our night instead. "So, where are we going tonight?"

"Nope." He smiles at me and shakes his head. "Still not telling you."

"Do you know?" I ask Erin, who just smiles and shakes her head.

"Beats me. You two have fun though," she says and waves us off.

I follow Tucker out to his truck, where he moves his jacket from the front seat to the bed—-where he also puts the bag he asked Nathan to pack for me. I am curious as to why I'll be needing a bag for the evening, but Nathan wouldn't let me peek.

"You ready?" he asks, with a smile that makes my heart do a flip.

"As I'll ever be without knowing where we're actually going," I say lightly, but really I'm dying to know.

"You'll know soon enough," he says as we pull out of the driveway. We fall into a comfortable silence, and after a while, it becomes obvious that it's going to take some time to get wherever it is we're going.. My thoughts wander back to two days ago, when everything was still fine and I didn't feel like a bomb was about to go off. I want to believe him, trust that Grace won't hate me forever, but I don't see her forgiving me anytime soon.

"And then, then he just took off running," Grace said, laughing. I roll back so I'm lying next to her on the floor. I've got tears in my eyes from laughing so hard.

"He did not just leave you? I know he's your boyfriend, but he's my brother, so I can kill him if you need me to."

"You don't need to kill him. But he just left me there! I was standing, soaking wet, and he left me," she says, still laughing. "Then, when he came back five minutes later, he was like, "Why are

you still standing here?" And I was like, "You left and I'm freezing," and he said, "Well, I wanted you to come with me."

"Oh my gosh, he's so dumb," I say, rolling over onto my stomach and propping myself up.

"Yes, but I really like him." She closes her eyes and hugs one of my pillows to her chest. "I'll just remember that next time he dares me to jump into the ocean with him, I'm supposed to follow him when he runs away, even though his pants were so waterlogged, I thought they were going to be around his ankles."

"That is a good part to remember."

"It was hilarious!"

There's a knock on my door, "Hey, Rosie. Doctor Barker called, she said that everything still looks good and that Lucy from your therapy group asked if she could have your number," Mom says all of that before she sees me, with Grace sitting beside me in my room. "Oh, hi, Grace."

My heart is beating wildly in my chest. "She can give Lucy my number."

"I'll let her know that's okay." She looks between me and Grace nervously. "Well, I'll let you girls get back to it." And then she leaves. I play with the carpet in front of me, wishing it wasn't so short, wishing I couldn't feel Grace's eyes on me.

"What was that about?" she asks in a quiet voice.

"Um, just following up... from my tests, back in January."

"That was three months ago." Grace sits up. "What's going on, Rosie?"

"Nothing, I'm fine," I assure her, because I am fine.

"Group therapy?" she asks, and I finally look at her, my chest bursting from holding it all in.

"Cancer group therapy." It all comes out in a rush, my heart nearly bursting out of my chest. "I had a tumor, but it's gone now. That's what I really had surgery for. But the tumor is gone, and I'm fine. There isn't cancer anywhere else, but I've been going to cancer group therapy because Doctor Barker thought it would help since I'd *been in remission so long and then I got a tumor. And I met a girl named Lucy who is sort of my new friend."*

She is quiet for a long minute and I look back at the carpet again. "You... wait... a tumor?"

"Yes." It comes out small.

"You knew about this in January?" I can't tell if she's mad or not.

"Yes."

"And you didn't tell me?" Her voice rises. She's definitely mad.

"No," I say, wanting to say more, but there's nothing else to say. I kept a secret, a big secret, for four months. I feel sick.

"Does Tucker know?" Then she laughs, as if she's figured it out. "Of course he doesn't, because he would be treating you even more like a queen than he already does if he'd known. And he would have told me."

"Yes," I say. "He knows."

"Gosh." She shakes her head. "You're really unbelievable."

I look at her. "What do you mean?"

Her face turns red and I'm not sure if she's about to scream or cry. "What do I mean?" she asks so quietly that it scares me. This is worse than screaming or crying. "I mean that my best friend, who I've known since I was TWO DAYS OLD, had a tumor and she didn't even tell me. She told her boyfriend, but not me!"

She's angry. Really angry.

I had planned this so differently; we'd talk about it in a few years and laugh about it. She wasn't supposed to be mad.

"I'm sorry," I whisper.

"Whatever." She stands abruptly and walks to my door. "I know that it was probably really scary," she says, looking at me. "Finding out you had a tumor again—but I can't believe that you let us think that everything was fine."

"Grace—" I know I should apologize, but the words catch in my throat.

"You should have told me." And then she leaves without another word.

I blink several times to focus on the road in front of me as Tucker turns off the freeway.

"Seriously, where are we going?" I ask. Now, it's not even to know what our surprise date is; it's to distract myself from the knot inside my stomach. *My best friend hates me.*

"You'll see!" He grabs my hand. "You'll like it."

"I guess I'll just have to trust you, then." I smile, pushing away the memories of Grace and the tumor. I just want to enjoy the night. I can enjoy this surprise and think about how to fix things between me and Grace tomorrow.

"I guess you will." He winks at me and then starts humming along to the song playing on the radio.

"Why aren't you talking?" I ask after a moment.

He lets out a laugh. "Mostly because I'm terrible at keeping secrets, so if I don't talk, I can't let where we're going slip. But we're almost there, so just a few more minutes."

We're both quiet when we pull up to a small cabin.

"Did Grace ever tell you about this place?" he asks as he turns off the engine; he doesn't move to get out though.

"Um, no," I say, wondering why Grace would ever tell me about a cabin up in the mountains. We've been best friends for all of our lives, but I know we still find out new things about each other all the time.

"It's our grandparents'. They still live down in Costa Mesa, but they wanted something in the mountains; not that you can really call this the mountains, but I guess it sort of works."

"And it's ours for the night?" I ask, my heart beating fast in my chest.

"And it's ours for the night." He looks nervous, too. "Originally, I wanted to spend the night in the bed of my truck, under the stars, because that seemed more romantic. Until Grace reminded me that it's still pretty chilly outside, and even though it's not as cold as I'm used to, it's too cold to stay out all night."

I shiver just thinking about it. "The cabin is a great idea."

He squeezes my hand three times and says, "Let's go inside."

I help him with the bags that are in the bed of his truck. "I had Nathan pack you a bag," he says, and his face is as red as a tomato when he says it. He unlocks the door and we head into the small cabin. There's a kitchen to our left, and to the right are two couches arranged around a fireplace.

"Wow, I haven't been up here since I was, like, six. I'll get a fire started." Soon, there's a roaring fire, and I settle in next to him on the floor as he unpacks the Chinese takeout we picked up down the road.

"So," I ask as I pull out a spring roll. "Why are you so embarrassed?"

His eyes go wide and he chokes on his water. "What?" he sputters.

"Your face has been the color of a cherry since we got out of the truck—why?" I'm in my favorite gray T-shirt dress, and I should be cold, but it's comfortable.

"Um... er." He coughs, clearing his throat.

"What is it?" We've always been able to talk about everything easily. It's weird to see him at a loss for words.

"I guess, uh, I just realized how this looks." Tucker lets the words out with another cough. "I take you up to this cabin, just the two of us, I, er... I'm not planning to do anything..." Now *my* face grows red.

This isn't something we've talked about before, and I honestly hadn't even been thinking about it.

"I, um." He lets out a laugh. "Why does this feel so awkward?"

I grab his hand. "It's not awkward, I promise."

"Right." He looks at me. "I care about you, a lot." His voice is softer now. "You've brought so much light into my life and I really care about you. I didn't bring you up here to have sex with you, even though a lot of guys our age would have jumped at the chance. But I'm not that guy and I think that's partially why my grandma gave me the key to this place. I know everything has moved pretty fast since we got together. I feel all of these feelings that are overwhelming, and if my mom were still here, she'd probably tell me that no teenagers could actually feel the way I do, but I do. I love you."

"I love you, too." I smile at him and then I lean forward to kiss him so he doesn't notice the tears in my eyes. His lips are warm, the heat from his embarrassment is fading, and he moves his hand to my neck, since my hair is up in a bun.

"I really, truly love you," he whispers against my lips and then he kisses me hard. This is the first time we've ever been truly alone. Even in his car, there are other people who could walk by at any moment. But this, right now, we're alone. I feel an ache in my body that I've never felt before; it's like I can't get close enough to him. I shift so that I'm in his lap, a movement that makes both of us gasp, and then he's kissing me again. He moves his hands up and down my back, and it feels like he's blazing a trail of fire with his fingertips. I lean into him more and hear him groan.

He pulls away from me slightly, our foreheads touching, and I notice how dark his eyes are. "Rosie." He breathes and I move to kiss him again. "Let's eat." His tone is serious, like he's trying hard to keep all that he's feeling out of his words. "Please."

I kiss him softly, one more time. This time, the passion and heat are still there, but it's slower. He keeps his hands still on my hips, moving only his lips. I ease away from him slowly, and settle back into my space on the floor next to him. I lean against the wall and put my legs across his.

Tucker grabs a carton of chicken and starts eating. I grab an eggroll and he meets my eye.

"I really like kissing you," I tell him, and he smiles.

"I like kissing you, too, darlin'." Then, we settle into a comfortable silence while we eat.

22

AFTER WE EAT, Tucker tends to the small fire and then plays a few songs on his guitar before we decide that it's late enough to go to bed.

I walk into the bedroom and drop my bag on the floor. "There's only one bed," I say, stupidly.

"Um, yeah. Is that alright?" He sounds nervous.

"Yeah, I mean, I assumed we would..." And now my face is red again. "Yes, it's great." I smile at him.

"I promise to keep my hands to myself," he tells me.

"Can we cuddle though?" I ask, innocently.

"Yeah, that's probably okay," he says. "The bathroom is through there." He points to the door on the left side of the room. "If you want to get ready first."

"Great." I pick up my bag and walk to the small bathroom. My cheeks are flushed from smiling, and laughing, and just being alone with him. It seems like there hasn't been a moment like this, ever. As I pull open my bag, I don't think about what my parents will say if they find out about this, or about Grace and what she's doing right now.

Instead, I pull out the 'pajamas' that Nathan packed for me.

"Seriously?" I say to myself as I hold up a pair of short shorts and a tank top that I rarely sleep in, even in the summer. It's freezing up at the cabin, and there doesn't seem to be any heat except for the fire we just put out in the other room. I cannot go out there dressed in this.

I wash my face and brush my teeth, pacing the tiny bathroom. My dress is comfortable, but I don't really want to sleep in it, so I change into the clothes Nathan packed for me and open the door.

"I did not pack my bag," I say, clutching it in front of me. I feel oddly exposed, even though the tank top is looser than most of my leotards. I watch him swallow as he looks at me, and then his eyes meet mine.

"Um." He clears his throat. "I might just kill your brother. I swear I told him to pack you something warm to sleep in because it gets cold." The words make me shiver as I register the cool air on my skin, but his eyes don't leave mine.

"It'll be fine, there's lots of blankets, right? And you'll just get to hold me all night." I trust him, and I trust what he promised, but the thought of spending the night in his arms thrills me. "That is what you wanted, right?"

"Mhm," is all he says. "I'm gonna go change."

I'm scrolling through social media when he comes out in a long-sleeved shirt and pajama pants. Much warmer and much more appropriate given the circumstances. "This cabin doesn't have heat, but it has Wi-Fi?" I ask, as he crawls under the covers and settles in next to me, not touching yet.

"I cannot explain my grandparents to you," he says, which makes me laugh.

"Well, it makes for a more interesting night." I put my phone on the nightstand and turn toward him. "Now what? I'm too wired to sleep." It's true—I don't want to stop talking, because I know the second it's quiet, I'll think about Grace being mad at me. "What do you want to do? Truth or Dare? Twenty questions? Make out?"

"As much as I'd love to make out with you, maybe later?" Tucker smiles at me.

"Twenty questions, it is. When did you first get into music?" I ask, and then I shiver in the cool air. It might be May, but in a small cabin like this in the mountains, it's a lot colder than by the beach. He wraps his arms around me, pulls me against his chest, and our legs tangle together. I rest my head on his pillow, a few inches away from his face.

"Whew, that's an easy one," he says breathlessly, like he can't believe I'm here in his arms. "Mom was always playing music. We didn't have a TV until I started middle school, so we just listened to music—mostly country. I was five when I asked for my first guitar. Mom got a second job to pay for lessons."

"Wow. That was really awesome of her." I don't have to wonder what it's like to have a mom who supports your dreams. I just wish sometimes that my mom didn't only live vicariously through me. It's so much pressure when you're living your own dream and your mom's. "Your turn."

"Um, okay." He thinks for a second. "What's your favorite dessert?"

"I'm more of a savory gal," I remind him, even though I know he already knows that I'd pick fries or chips or popcorn over anything sweet. "But, I really, really love Erin's cinnamon rolls, so I'm really looking forward to one of those tomorrow morning. If you could go anywhere in the world, where would you go?"

"I'm right where I want to be." He brushes his nose against mine. "But I'd love to go back to Nashville after graduation if I can. I'd love to show it to you."

"I'd like that," I say honestly, and push away the thoughts of *when* that could happen. We're going to graduate soon, and then he'll start touring and I'll be heading to Paris.

"Why do you look sad?" he asks me.

"Do I?" I ask. "I wasn't meaning to look sad. It's been a long week, I'm tired, but trust me, I'm not sad to be here with you. And that totally counts as your question."

"Fair enough," he says.

"What's something you've always wanted to do?" I ask him.

"Another easy one, darlin'." He winks at me. "Get a record deal."

"You'll definitely do that someday," I say, and I hope he can tell how much I believe in him; how much I know that he's going to get everything he wants. "You're going to be famous, I can just feel it in my bones."

"Thank you," he says quietly. "What's one thing you want to do before you die?" I freeze in his arms. "Sorry, I know that's a rough question considering your past with cancer and all, but you're here still, and fine, and I'm still fine, but I've been thinking about that lately. Especially since you told me about the tumor."

I nod, forcing myself to be calm and collected. I am fine. I'm alive and well. "I know I could say something about dance," I start and my voice cracks—I don't know why I'm so emotional about this. "But I don't think that'd be a truthful answer. I think I'd love to see The Nutcracker again, on a stage. I haven't seen it in years, partially because I was in it for about four years and then they haven't shown it at any local theaters the past few years. But I'd love to see it again. And I'd love to spend at least one more night with you."

"Well, it's a good thing we've got a lot of time together. I'd love to see The Nutcracker with you. And maybe we can make this happen again," he says, and his eyes are dark as he stares down at me. I kiss him. Tucker is frozen at first, but then he moves, pulling me closer to him. My top shifts and his hands brush the skin of my lower back, which makes him pull me even closer. I kiss him harder.

I run my hands through his hair, full of desire. He slows his lips and pulls away slightly.

"Whoa." He lets out a shaky breath, and when I lean in to kiss him again, it's like he can't refuse. I slip a hand up the back of his shirt, feeling his cool skin against my flaming fingers, and he lets out a groan, which makes me smile, and I pull him closer when his phone rings.

"Leave it," I say, kissing his neck, but he's already reaching for his phone. I see the name on the screen. It's Erin.

"Can't, it's Aunt Erin," he says, and I move away just enough so he can answer the call. "Hello?"

I can hear her over the speaker because it's so quiet in the cabin.

"Tucker," she starts, and I know whatever she has to say next won't be good based on her stern tone. "Grace told me where you took Rosie tonight. I've called Catherine and she's on her way over here." I bury my face in my hands. I should have guessed that *this* is what she would do. She'd tell my mom about my first ever romantic getaway, if that's actually what this is.

"Crap." He sits up. "I'm so sorry. I promise my intentions are pure. We weren't, we aren't..." I grab his free hand to let him know that I'm here with him.

"It doesn't matter, Tucker, I think the two of you should come home," I hear Erin say. "You haven't been drinking, right?"

"No, Erin." He sounds like a little kid who just got in trouble for stealing cookies.

"I'll see you in a couple hours," she says before ending the call, and Tucker sets his phone on the bed in front of him.

"I'm so sorry, Rosie. This is all my fault, I'm so sorry."

My chest feels heavy—this was supposed to be our night, just us for once. And even though I didn't know about it until we got here, I wanted this for us.

"Hey." I crawl closer to him, putting my hand on his face so he has to look at me. "It was a perfect few hours."

"You sure?"

"I'm sure." I give him a quick kiss before jumping out of bed and pulling on my dress over my pajamas.

I help him grab the few things we brought and make sure—again—that the fire is completely out, before we walk out and he locks the door behind us.

The wind has picked up and I'm shaking by the time we get into his truck, so I climb into the middle seat and sit as close as I can to him until the heat kicks on. I've got my head on his shoulder and our hands in my lap.

"It's all going to be okay," I repeat several times, both to assure him, and also myself.

"Why would she do this?" he asks when we are out of the canyon. I know who he's talking about.

"Um," I say. "I'm guessing she's going to be mad at me forever for not telling her about the tumor."

"That's dumb," he says. "I mean, I guess I get that she's mad, but... you're fine, so it's not that big of a deal."

I don't deserve his forgiveness. Grace has every right to be mad at me; I didn't tell her the truth for months, even after telling Tucker. That wasn't fair to her, and I just kept putting it off until it was too late.

"So, this is sort of my fault that our night was ruined," I say glumly.

"No, Rosie, it's not your fault. She didn't have to do this to get back at you."

"Yeah, I'm still sorry."

"No, don't be." He presses a quick kiss into my hair. "Like you said, it was a perfect few hours together."

"Yeah." I let out a quiet sigh and enjoy the last couple of hours I have alone with him, since I don't know what awaits us at home.

<h1 style="text-align:center">23</h1>

"IT'S GOING TO BE OKAY." I'm still attempting to reassure both of us as we pull off the freeway and into our neighborhood. We were both pretty quiet the whole way home, which made the drive feel even longer. Tucker seems nervous, like he only planned for a night away, and didn't actually think it all the way through. Not that I did either, even though I didn't know where we were going. Now it seems like it probably wasn't his best idea, even though I'm grateful for the alone time.

I don't actually know what will happen when we get home. Mom might forgive me because of the whole tumor thing, but I really don't want her to say anything in front of Tucker.

"I hope so." His knuckles are white on the steering wheel. I wish I could kiss him again, get him to relax. My body goes warm, thinking about the kiss that got interrupted. I want to kiss him like that again. But there isn't time when we pull into the driveway.

It's way past midnight, but all the lights are on at Tucker's house. I'm already exhausted and not ready to have a shouting match with Mom, which is bound to happen. My body feels like it's going to collapse and my mind won't stop running. He smashes his lips against mine before we climb out of the truck; it's urgent and messy, like we both know we don't have enough time. Because it feels like there isn't enough time. I want to linger, but he pulls away too soon.

"It's going to be okay," I whisper again, and I take his hand as we walk up to the front door. "Ready?"

"Not really, no. You'd think this would be a little less scary since my mom isn't here to see this, but your mom kind of freaks me out."

I let out a small, nervous laugh. "Me too, honestly."

He squeezes my hand three times and then opens the door. Mom and Erin are talking softly on the couch. Nathan is asleep on the floor and Grace is curled up on her dad's oversized chair, scrolling on her phone.

Mom looks worried and furious.

"You are in so much trouble," she whisper-yells, if that's a thing, but I know she's tired and doesn't want to wake Nathan up yet. "Lying about this?"

"I didn't know, and then when I did, I just wanted to enjoy it. We didn't even do anything." I cling to Tucker's hand since it's the only thing really keeping me grounded right now.

"You still went," Mom hisses at me. "You still were going to spend the night with him. And you." She turns to Tucker and I take a step closer to him.

"I'm sorry, Catherine," he says sincerely, and I see Mom's eyes soften slightly, but I know she's not going to back down. "I wasn't thinking..."

"You're right, you weren't thinking. You are both too young to be having sex," she says.

"Mom." I know my face is bright red. "That wasn't what happened. Or what was going to happen."

"We just wanted some time alone." His face is also pink, and his ears are bright red. "I am sorry."

Mom lets out a long sigh. "It was a stupid idea. Both of you might be eighteen, but that doesn't make you adults."

I look straight at her; there's a lot I want to say, but nothing I want to say in front of Tucker. We may not have graduated from high school yet, but technically, we *are* adults. Doesn't that mean we should be able to make our own choices?

"Go upstairs, get some sleep," Mom says quietly, surprising both of us. "In separate rooms obviously, but we'll talk more in the morning." Then Mom hugs me, which makes Tucker's eyes go wide. I know mine must look just like his. Mom doesn't do hugs, so I have no idea what's happening. But before I can register the hug, she releases me and gives me a nudge in the direction of the stairs.

I head up to Grace's bedroom and Tucker stays behind while Erin whispers to him in hushed tones at the bottom of the stairs. I wait in the doorway for Erin's door to close downstairs, then I'm down the hall and going down the stairs, where I meet him.

"What did she say?" I ask, my hands on his shoulders.

"That it wasn't my smartest move, which she might be right about."

"But it was a good night, and it gave me something to look forward to in the future," I whisper.

His eyes darken.

There are so many things I'd like to do with him, but exhaustion has hit. "I am tired, though."

His eyes clear. "Me too. I'll see you in the morning?"

"I'll be here," I say, and he kisses me softly before heading back downstairs. I sink into Grace's bed and I'm asleep in minutes.

Grace is watching *Grey's Anatomy* on her laptop when I wake up.

"Morning," she says without looking at me. The sinking feeling in my gut that's been there for days hits full force again.

"I'm sorry for not telling you," I finally get the words out.

"I don't really care," she says, still watching her show and not looking at me. "But why did you tell him and not me?"

"It just came out after the Valentine's Dance, and even though I've had so many opportunities to tell you, I just couldn't get the words out. I didn't want to be the girl with cancer again." She and I have always been friends, but when I was sick the first time, she got closer with other girls. And even though I was young, I understood. I was in the hospital, and she needed new friends. But it still stung. Still stings. I think that's part of why I didn't tell her; I didn't want to lose her again.

"Rosie." She slams her laptop shut. "This isn't like last time."

I sigh. Of course she knows what I'm thinking. We had plenty of chats about everything after I was in remission. "I know."

"Obviously you don't, or you would have told me."

"I'm sorry I didn't tell you." My voice sounds small. "I should have, and you have every right to be mad at me. But did you have to do this? Tell our moms about where Tucker and I were last night?"

She looks a little guilty. "You're my best friend, we're supposed to tell each other things."

"You didn't tell me about you and Nathan. I wasn't mad about that, just surprised."

"Dating your brother and finding out you had a tumor are two completely separate things," she huffs out.

My chest is tight. I hate when we argue. But we've both kept secrets that we should have been open about. I know that now.

"Can we finish this conversation later? I know we need to hash this all out, but my mom's gonna ground me for literally the rest of my life, so, ya know. I can't really add more on top of that." She gives me a look that says *You're being an idiot.* But I don't say anything else.

"You're just mad that I ruined your night."

"Yeah, I am." I stand, pulling my hair into a ponytail as I pace the room. "You couldn't let us have one night together?"

She rolls her eyes, and I clench my teeth.

"It's not like you guys aren't going to have more nights together. He's in love with you. I didn't ruin anything."

Except she did. Mom is going to kill me. Despite her being weirdly nice last night, I know that once I go downstairs to talk to her again, she's going to let all hell break loose and accuse me of being just like her.

"You did, though," I whisper.

"Knock-knock," Nathan says as he opens the door. "Mom's back, and she's ready to talk. Erin made cinnamon rolls."

My stomach twists.

Even though it was Tucker's idea, I still went with him. She may think I deserve whatever punishment she's about to dole out, but I'm eighteen now. I graduate in a month. I can make my own choices.

Nathan and Grace don't follow me downstairs. Tucker's already sitting at the kitchen table, nursing a cup of Erin's famous hot chocolate. She hands me a mug as I slide onto the bench next to him.

He puts a hand on my leg and looks at me with apologetic eyes. "It's okay," I whisper. "No regrets." He nods and we both look at my mom, who sits down across from us, and Erin next to her.

Mom looks calm as she looks at both of us. "I'm disappointed in you, both of you," she says, and I wish she'd yell instead of talking so softly. "After talking to Erin, though, I guess I understand a little more. I was a young teenager in love once, too. But there are still going to be consequences," she says, and both Tucker and I nod. My resolve from a few moments ago? Completely gone. I don't know if I'll ever be able to stand up to her.

"Rosie, you'll work the front desk at the studio right after school for two hours instead of one, every day for the next month. And no phone for two weeks." I slide my phone across the table, and she gives me an appreciative look for not fighting. I don't want to get into this with her. She doesn't trust me, and I don't know if she ever will.

"As for you." Erin clasps her hands in front of her on the table as she looks at Tucker. "I talked to your mom this morning. She said she'll call you later, but said that she's fine with whatever punishment I deem fit, as you live in my house. I can assume most of this was all teenage hormones and caring for each other. That being said, the two of you do need to be careful. So, for the next couple of weeks, I want you to have a chaperone: me, Grace, Nathan, Kenny, or Micah. Just to help things simmer down a bit. Deal?"

"Deal," he says. "Can we go now?"

"Yup, as long as there's someone else with you." I hate this new rule more than I hate not having my phone, but we'll just have to live with it. We head up to Grace's room, where Nathan and Grace are waiting for us.

"Well?"

"Mom wasn't as mad as I thought," I say, and Grace looks disappointed.

"You should have seen her last night," Nathan tells us. "She was livid."

"My mom talked her down," Grace says, still frowning. "So what's the punishment?"

"I don't have a phone for the next few weeks and I have to work the front desk at the studio." Which is more of a punishment than I'd like to admit. I don't mind being in the studio, but working the front desk is the worst job because you have to deal with all the crazy dance moms. I already have a mom who is a coach *and* a mom. I hate having to talk to the other moms. And it'll just be more time not dancing while I'm there.

"And one of you gets to be our third wheel for the rest of time," he says, and Grace groans.

"Noooo... that's punishment for *us*." Grace pulls a pillow over her face. "Just keep it... well, not gross?"

"We can do that," I say, and suddenly feel lightheaded. My stomach is in anxious knots as I wonder why, so I sit on the bed as quickly as I can, but slow enough to not raise anyone's suspicion. But Nathan knows me too well, and he's watching me carefully. "Disney marathon today?" I ask to move the attention away from me.

"YES!" Grace jumps up so quickly that I wonder if she's forgiven me. But after the fight we just had, I know this is far from over. "We could watch all day since you all are already here. We'll get through so many movies! I'll go see if I can bribe Micah to play Mario Kart on a different TV."

"I'm gonna go shower, but I'll be back." Tucker waves and winks at me before heading out the door.

"Are you okay?" Nathan asks as soon as they're both gone.

I nod. "Just a little lightheaded, probably from all the excitement of the morning. I also haven't had anything to eat yet."

"Okay," he says, but I know he doesn't believe me. I don't even believe me. But I'm fine, it was just one tumor. I'm clear.

"I'm really okay." I give him a hug. "Was Mom really mad?"

"I thought she was going to be that dark shade of purple forever. I don't know if she was more mad about the idea that the two of you might have, well, ya know, or the fact that you had gone off without telling her. I know she was mad, but I think she was scared."

"I know."

"And we almost lost you once before, but this time..." Nathan trails off. This time is different, and we all know it.

"This time I just had a tumor," I try to say brightly. "And I'm gonna be fine. No one is almost losing me, and I'm not having sex, so my dance career isn't on the line. Plus, if I was, there is this thing called birth control." Nathan shudders at this information. "I am sorry for freaking everyone out. I'll apologize again to Mom. And not ask for my phone back until next week."

"You can live without social media for a week," Nathan says, rolling his eyes.

"But I won't be able to text Tucker."

"You don't have to live in isolation. You'll still see him at school, and all day today, because now, thanks to you, we're watching movies all day. Grace and I did have other plans."

"She seemed up for a movie day."

"I think she's still mad at you for not telling her about the tumor, but I think she wants to forgive you and Disney movies are her love language." Nathan says it like I've asked him to pull out his teeth one by one. "But I'm glad she knows. Are you sure you're okay?" he asks as I sink onto the bed a little more. I need to eat something. Last night wiped me out.

"She is still mad at me. And don't baby me, I'm okay, I was just up super late," I say because I'm exhausted from the long night. "And I probably just need something to eat."

"This has been hard for me, too," he says, and he leaves before I have a chance to respond. I sit in the middle of the room, wondering when things got so weird between me and my twin—the person I've always been the closest to. I knew things would change a little as we got older, but I feel like there's a void between us and I want to fix it.

journal entries - present day

MAY *3*

Dear Journal,

I've been doing a lot of thinking lately. About what Lucy said at group therapy and then the conversation I had with my dad, and I guess this is where I'm at:

Things in life happen to all of us and sometimes it really, really sucks. And there is this big God somewhere (at least, I think there is, maybe, but I think there's some peace I find in believing in that) but He doesn't always take the pain away from us. I still don't understand why.

I still don't understand why I had to get cancer again or why Lucy keeps having to have surgery. I don't understand why Tucker's dad is such a loser or why most people don't want to live by the ocean—okay, they don't have to come live here, there's already a ton of people here so...

So, I feel like I'm still in the same spot I was.

Lucy called me the other day and we talked for a little while, and she invited me to come visit her on Sunday next week to chat more about what she shared in therapy. Maybe I'll get some more answers there.

Okay, now I feel like I should/want to write a letter to him about some things I've been thinking about that I just want to share with him.

Love, Rosie

Dear Tucker,

My body still seems so weak, I haven't been dancing or training like I was before my surgery. I'm still taking it slow, but it's killing me.

I am really grateful that I only had a tumor because cancer is exhausting. Surgery was exhausting.

But, it's been 4 months that we've been together :)

I've never really thought about soulmates or if I believed in them or not. Not even with my parents, but they were definitely meant for each other. Dad loves Mom so much, and while most of the time Mom is stuck in ballet mode, she's obsessed with Dad, too.

But then—then there's us.

It's always been you for me, which is why I fought so hard against it.

I dated Shawn as a distraction. We never even kissed. It wasn't like that—more of a business contract, which I know when you and Grace learn about that you'll really hate me. So why am I writing it in this letter? Probably because I'll never give it to you, so it really doesn't matter.

When I met you, everything changed. I don't think I realized it at that moment though. It was one of those seemingly insignificant moments at the time. You know the ones—you meet someone new, or you make the choice to go down one road instead of the road you usually take. It doesn't seem like a big deal until someone runs a red light.

I feel like that's what meeting you was like. It was at that moment that everything shifted, even though I didn't know it yet.

But the thing about soulmates, and I've been thinking about this a lot—the thing about soulmates is that they could be anyone. The friend you've had forever or maybe the person you met for the first time today. Sometimes a soulmate looks like a best friend, but sometimes, if you're lucky, you get to fall in love with your person, the one that lights you up and fills you up with this joy that you can't even explain. They are the ones who understand you better than anyone else in the entire world. And you get to love them and be loved by them every single day.

I'm so grateful I get to be loved by you, even if soulmates aren't a thing. I hope you're right and that we get to have forever, cause that sounds pretty great.

I love you.

Love, Rosie

24

WE'RE ALL at the beach. Nathan, Grace, Tucker, and me. Tucker's got his arm around me and Grace is pretending to be fine, even though I know she's still mad at me. Everything feels almost normal.

It was Grace's idea to spend the night at the beach. She still wants to hang out, but there's an underlying tension between the two of us, and the last time I tried to bring it up, she brushed me off and said everything was fine. But it doesn't feel fine. I want everything to be alright between us, but I don't know what else I can do to fix the chasm I created.

We have two weeks until graduation and it is finally feeling warmer. We loaded up the back of Tucker's truck with blankets and pillows and a ton of snacks. Even though it's been warm during the day, it still gets pretty cool at night.

I think Mom only said yes because she didn't want to argue with Dad when Nathan asked him.

"Want to get in the water?" Grace asks me.

"Yeah," I answer, even though I don't really want to get in the freezing water, but I'm trying to do what I can to get back in her good graces after lying about the tumor.

Tucker moves his arm from around me so that I can get up; I look out at the dark water to avoid looking at Grace as we head toward the waves. Once I figure out how to fix things between us, I'll try to talk to her again, one-on-one. Until then, we'll still hang out as a group, but I think everyone can feel how awkward it is right now.

Growing up near the ocean is something I never take for granted. Maybe it's because of Mom or the stories she tells about Dad.

Dad loves the water.

He's an artist by nature, but he's up at the crack of dawn almost every day when the weather's good, out on the waves. Mom was sad at first that neither Nathan or I had any interest in surfing, but I still love the ocean. She says I get that from Dad.

I take a deep breath of the salty air; the sound of the waves is calming. Back and forth, back and forth as the water tickles my toes. That's as far as I want to get in, just to my ankles. The sun has barely set, so the sky is on fire with pinks, oranges, and purples and the ocean is already dark.

"I love the beach," I say, taking in another deep breath. There isn't anything quite like it—the smell of the ocean and the salt in the air that leaves your hair and skin a little grimy if you stay out too long.

"I'm hungry," Nathan says from behind us, even though we've been eating all the food we brought since we got to the beach two hours ago. Nathan always seems to be hungry.

Tucker wraps his arms around me, pulling me against his back as the cold waves swirl against our feet. He presses his lips into my hair.

We head back to the blanket, where my brother opens another bag of chips.

"We should play Truth or Dare," Grace announces as she tucks her legs underneath her, criss-cross applesauce. Nathan and Tucker both groan.

"Why?" Tucker asks. "We already all know each other, so truth isn't even all that fun."

"So pick dare." Grace shrugs. "Dares are more fun anyway."

"Why don't we play something else?" Nathan suggests.

"Like what?" she asks, and I've never been more grateful for Nathan than in this moment. I know exactly what Grace would ask me to do, whether I pick a truth or a dare. She'll want to call me out on my lie. I know she's mad at me, but I think she's also mad at Tucker for not being mad when I told him the truth.

"Like nothing," Nathan says and I let out a nervous laugh. Grace narrows her eyes at me and I shiver.

Tucker pulls me closer to him, even though I'm not shivering from the cold.

"We could make a bucket list," I say suddenly, and I feel everything shift in the air.

"We don't need to do that," Grace says at the same time Nathan asks, "Do you really think that's a good idea?"

I feel Tucker's eyes on me.

"Why not?" I ask. "It can be for all of us. Life is short. We should do the things we want to do before we die. Or maybe just before we all go our separate ways in the fall?"

Everyone is quiet, and the roar of the dark waves calms me. Even though I'm not dying, Nathan is looking at me like I might. Grace is still glaring.

I hoped that she would be excited for a bucket list. She tried to get me to make one a few summers ago, but I told her they were dumb. Why make a list of things you want to do before you die? Why not just do them?

Now I wish I had, because these days, time is feeling too short. I feel as though I'm on borrowed time, even though at my last scan, everything still looked good.

"Come on, it will be fun." I move to my knees and pull out my phone. I open the notes app, and type, **Our Bucket List,** at the top.

"Who's first?" I ask. Tucker is looking at me with a confused expression on his face. I can't look at Nathan because he's looking at me like I'm a piece of glass that's about to break, so I look at Grace.

"Get a tattoo," she says, and she's no longer glaring at me.

"You want a tattoo?" Tucker asks, surprised.

"Yeah, I actually do," she tells him. "At some point, so maybe not this summer, but put it on the list."

I type it out.

"I told Tucker a couple of months ago that I'd love to see The Nutcracker again," I say and type it out.

"I'd like to go on an international tour someday," Tucker says quietly.

"You will!" I bump my shoulder with his.

"I want to solve a medical mystery," Nathan says.

"Good, good, this is good," I say. "The bigger the better, right?"

"How about spending a night under the stars?"

Grace looks at Tucker like he's stated the most obvious thing. "Um, like we're doing right now?"

"I guess that's true," Tucker says. "But hey, we can cross one thing off the list!"

"I'd love to go on a road trip together," Nathan says.

"That would be so fun," I say. "We could do that this summer, before I go to Paris and Tucker goes on tour and you go to school."

"Let's do it," Tucker says.

"I think Rosie should tell Tucker the truth," Grace says suddenly, and my stomach drops. No, not like this. She can't be doing this. Is she really still that mad at me?

Tucker freezes behind me. "Tell me the truth about what?"

I'm about to answer when my phone rings; it's Mom. "Give me a sec." Nathan's eyes are wide on me as I stand to move away and answer her call.

I hear Tucker ask, "What does she need to tell me the truth about? I know about the tumor."

Grace just huffs. Why is she trying to stir up drama? Tucker knows everything now.

"Hello," I say into the phone.

"Oh, good, Rosie. I'm so glad you picked up," Mom says, concern lacing her voice.

"Yeah?"

"Two things," she says. "First, Doctor Barker called. She said that something abnormal came back with your bloodwork, something they missed before."

My heart sinks. "Okay," is all I can manage to say.

"Are you sitting?" Mom asks next. "Because there's more."

"No."

"You probably should," she says gently. I don't know if I've ever heard her sound so—so caring. That scares me more than anything.

"Okay," I tell her, but remain standing.

"Honey, I'm so sorry," she says. "But Doctor Barker said that Lucy's parents wanted her to tell us that Lucy passed last night."

The whole world goes fuzzy, like all the air has been sucked into a vacuum. My head spins.

"But I just talked to her yesterday morning. We were going to have lunch in her room on Sunday," I say, in shock.

"I know, sweetie."

"Do you know what happened?"

"A little. I spoke with Doctor Barker and then with Lucy's mom for a moment. They were in surgery, trying to remove the tumor—" Mom says, but I interrupt.

"But they said that they couldn't do that, that trying that would kill her." I'm vaguely aware that I'm bordering on hysteria. Nathan's face materializes in front of mine, but I shake my head and turn away, walking closer to the dark water.

"I know, Rosie, but her mom said she was having too many

seizures and they had to try it," Mom says. "She knew the risks. Her mom said she'll let me know about the funeral once the arrangements have been made."

"Why would they do the surgery?" I scream into the phone. "They knew it could kill her."

"Oh, Rosie," Mom says, and I want to throw my phone in the ocean. Lucy can't be dead. She was the only friend who sort of understood what I was going through, and she was supposed to answer my questions.

"Thanks for telling me," I say, suddenly angry. I hang up before she can say anything else, folding my arms tightly against my chest, as if that will fix everything.

"Rosie?" I hear my twin ask tentatively.

"What?" I snap.

"What did Mom say?" His voice is soothing and gentle, but that only makes the tears come faster and harder.

"Lucy's gone," I cry. I'm still processing the part about the abnormality, and I won't share anything until we know for sure. But Lucy is gone; I start to shake and I'm startled when arms come around me. I feel Tucker's warm body behind mine.

"Who's Lucy?" I'm not sure if he's asking me or Nathan, but I can't find the words to respond.

"A girl that Rosie met during group therapy," Nathan tells him.

"Therapy?" Tucker asks like it's the first time he's heard about it, because it is the first time he's heard about it. I told him about the tumor, but never told him about therapy. Probably because I wasn't sure what I'd say, because I didn't know what I was feeling about everything we talked about in therapy and with Lucy.

"Cancer therapy," I whisper, then turn to look at him.

His eyes grow wide with concern. "You didn't tell me about therapy. "

"I had a tumor," I say, tears still falling down my face, but now I'm not sure they're all still for Lucy.

"I know." Tucker's face twists in confusion. "Who's Lucy?"

"A girl I met at therapy," I whisper. A girl who's gone now. "My doctor told my mom that there's something abnormal about my bloodwork, but they need to do more tests to know what it is."

Tucker takes a step back from me, and I miss his warmth almost immediately,

"What?" Nathan asks, startled.

"I have to go in for more tests soon," I tell them, still watching Tucker, who stands a step away from me, as tears slide down my face. "I need you, I can't go through this again without you."

Tucker is shaking his head in disbelief; he opens his mouth, then closes it again. His eyes meet mine again and I'm surprised to see tears.

"Please," I whisper. He takes a step closer to me.

"I love you, Rosie." He tucks some of my hair behind my ear, his eyes flitting over my face like he's trying to memorize me. "But I..." He takes a shaky breath. "I need some time."

A sob escapes me. "What?"

He takes a step back. "I just need some time to think. Keep me posted on the test results, okay?"

"Tucker—" I reach for him, but he takes another step back.

"I can't..." His eyes looked pained, like he knows this is a mistake, but he's doing it anyway.

"I don't want you to leave," I say. Someone wraps their arms around my shoulders and I sink against them. I don't know if it's Grace or Nathan, but I need them. If Tucker walks away, I need someone.

"I'm not leaving," he says. "I just need some space."

And then he's gone, and I break down on the beach.

journal entries - present day

MAY *10*

Dear Journal,

I wouldn't be surprised if Tucker hates me. He hasn't responded to any of my calls or texts, and when I stopped by yesterday morning before going to the hospital for more tests and scans, Erin said he didn't want to talk to me or anyone. I don't know what to do. He said he needed space, but he completely walked away. Who does that? I need him right now, but he can't seem to handle the idea of having a sick girlfriend. :(

On the bright side (is there a bright side to your boyfriend not talking to you?) Grace has officially forgiven me and she's come over every day that I'm not at the studio. I can finally dance again—even if it's not as intense as before, at least I'm dancing. For now.

Nathan is also talking to me more. The shift was so small that I almost didn't notice until he drove us to school today and I realized we talked the whole time instead of just listening to the music.

Maybe I should have just told the truth from the beginning. I was so afraid of losing Tucker and Grace that I kept my tumor from them, but in a way, I lost both of them.

Then there's Lucy. I'm not ready to talk about it yet. Any time I think about her (like now) I start crying. Which makes me feel a little dumb. I barely knew her and yet...

I don't know if Tucker and I will be okay, which I really really hate. I miss him so much. I know I messed up. I don't know how to make it right.

Love, Rosie

May 12

Dear Journal,

Doctor Barker called today. She said we have to go in. I don't think that's a good thing. If it was good news, she would have told us over the phone.

I really want to talk to Tucker about this, but he won't answer any of my calls or texts. I see him at school, but mostly, he avoids me. I hate this so much.

Love, Rosie

25

ALL I CAN HEAR IS white noise. After Doctor Barker said that I have a tumor growing in the exact same place as Lucy's, I've gone numb. After blood tests confirmed there was cancer growing somewhere in my body, they did a full-body scan and found the tumor.

Mom cried.

Surgery might be a short-term fix, like it was for Lucy, but with how aggressive this kind of tumor is, Doctor Barker doesn't think that surgery is going to be the only option this time. There will be radiation, possibly chemotherapy, and surgery.

I have cancer. I have cancer. I have cancer. I feel like I'm trying to swim through the words. How do I have cancer? How is it back? How is it so bad? Do I really have a death sentence now?

"Do we know how much time she has?" Dad's question snaps me back to reality, but Doctor Barker shakes her head.

"We'll have a better estimate of that in a few weeks, after we see how Rosie responds to the treatments; but even then, it will be hard to know, just like with Lucy." She smiles sadly at us. "I am so sorry."

Nathan is sitting on the floor of the small hospital room,

hugging his knees to his chest. Mom's got her head in her hands and Dad is rubbing her back. I'm sitting frozen on the bed. I'm still in my normal clothes, since I'm not checked in at the moment, and I want to cry, but I can't seem to make the tears come.

Mostly I feel empty.

I want to feel angry. Angry that they didn't catch this before, angry that cancer has been possibly growing inside my body for months, since my first surgery, and we could have been fighting it all along.

But I feel nothing.

We're all quiet on the drive home, and when we get there, I say that I'm tired and I'll be in my room if anyone needs me. As I shut my door and crawl straight into bed, I pull my phone out of my nightstand. Still nothing.

> Hey, Tuck. I don't know how you're feeling but I miss you and I got some news from the doctor, which you said you wanted to know. Can we talk?
>
> Please?

"Can I come in?" I put my phone face down on my nightstand and motion for Nathan to come into my room. "How're you holding up?"

"Fine, I guess," I say. I don't know how I feel, I just know that I'd feel better if Tucker and I were on talking terms. Because even when we weren't together, we still texted and talked nearly every day.

"I'm sorry, Rosie." He sinks onto my bed next to me, our heads nearly brushing on the pillow. "I mean, I'd be upset, too, if the person I loved was sick. But I wouldn't walk away."

I don't have a response for that; I didn't think Tucker would walk away either. But I guess it really is too much to handle. I'd walk away if I could, if it wasn't my life.

I squeeze his hand.

"I'm scared." Nathan's whisper is barely audible.

Me too. "Of what?" I ask instead.

"Of being alone. Of losing you. I don't know if I can handle it." I sit up and wrap my arms around him. I want to say that we don't know that anyone is going to lose me. We don't know yet if the treatment will work or what stage my cancer is really at until they do a biopsy of the tumor, which they're doing tomorrow. But even with that, it doesn't matter because of the placement. I really am on limited time now, just like Lucy was. But I don't know what I'd do without Nathan, so I can't even fathom what he's feeling right now.

"You take it one day at a time," I say, trying to reassure myself just as much as him. Because the truth is, I'm scared of dying. It's the one thing that we don't really know anything about. Will I just stop being? Will part of me go somewhere else? We don't have answers and that terrifies me. "You just take it one day at a time and surround yourself with a lot of people who love you."

Nathan sniffles and nods. "I'm not ready to lose you."

"Me either." I choke on the words because I'll be losing him, too, if that's what happens in the end. "But you won't be alone." That, at least, gives me comfort.

"It won't be the same," he says quietly. "A life without you would feel too empty." I don't know how to respond to that. We've never really had someone close to us die; I don't know how to comfort my twin.

"You should try to talk to Tucker," he says finally.

"I have been trying," I say. "I think he's just going to avoid me forever."

Nathan shakes his head. "He won't, he cares about you too much. You two need to talk. You have to tell him about today. He still loves you, and I know he misses you. You two are, like, meant for each other, and even if you've got this crazy tumor, that doesn't mean you aren't supposed to be together."

"Since when do you believe in soulmates?"

"I didn't call it that, but that is a word for it. It's just..." Nathan pauses, as if trying to figure out the right words to say. "When the two of you are together, everything seems right in the world. I don't know how to explain it. I need him to explain it, he's the one that really believes in all the soulmates and one true love stuff. But you two are just right for each other. So you should go talk to him."

"He won't even text me back." I really *want* to go talk to Tucker. Even if we never hold hands or kiss again, I need him to be my friend again.

"Go see him."

"What if he's not home?"

"Then wait for him."

"Why are you so adamant about this? Why now?" I ask.

Nathan's blue eyes peer into mine. "Because I think you're going to need him by your side this time, and I think he's going to want to be there, even if he's scared right now."

I nod, because it's true. I don't want to do this without Tucker.

"Let's go now." Nathan squeezes my knee. "I'll drive you over."

I smile at him. "But you hate driving." He shrugs as if to say, *but I'll do it for you, just this once.*

Tucker isn't home when we get there, but I'm too emotional to hang out with Nathan and Grace. Grace's family is all out doing something fun, but I just want to be alone. Nathan and Grace head downstairs to watch a movie while I wait in Tucker's room. I'm exhausted from the news of today, so I curl up in his blankets, hoping to just rest until he gets home.

26

"ROSIE."

I roll away from the voice; I do not want to get up yet. Why is Mom waking me up for school? She hasn't done that in years.

"Rosie," the voice says again, and this time I'm awake enough to realize that it's Grace who's standing above me.

"What's going on?" I ask groggily. I sit up, remembering that Nathan and I came over to see Tucker. I glance at the alarm clock on top of his desk at the other side of the room. "It's one in the morning?"

I finally look at her; she's still dressed and she looks like she's been crying. "What's going on?"

"Nathan told me," she says first, and I open my arms to give her a hug. She crawls onto the tiny twin bed next to me and I hold her while she cries, but I still can't will the tears to come, even though I can feel the emotion building up inside me.

"This time I won't keep any secrets from you," I promise, and she nods, then abruptly sits up.

"There's something else you should know." She's still got her arms around me in an awkward hug that's making me sit weird, but I don't move. She looks so serious.

"What?" I ask nervously.

"Tucker's gone," she says, and it takes a few moments for the words to sink in.

"What do you mean?" I ask, hoping I don't sound as panicked as I feel.

"He left a note on the counter, sometime last night or early this morning. Said he's going back home to stay with his mom for a while and work on his music in Nashville."

My stomach drops. "He... he just left?" I ask, shaking my head. This can't be happening. He wouldn't just leave. "Why would he do that? Why would he just leave without saying goodbye?"

"I don't know." She gives me another tight hug, but I jerk out of her embrace. I stand in the middle of his room and look around, my heart pounding in my chest.

His closet door is open and I can see that some of his clothes are gone. I turn to the corner where his guitar always sits—it's gone. I was too tired to notice before.

"He left." I sink down onto the floor, anger still pulsing through me. "He actually left." Then, for the first time since I found out that Lucy died, I weep.

When Lucy's mom calls the next morning to give us the details for Lucy's funeral, Grace and Nathan promise me they'll be there to hold my hand the whole time. I feel like a zombie as we get ready the next day and drive up to her hometown, Newport Beach. I didn't even know where she lived. There's so much I didn't know about her, and so much I'll never know now.

Dad drives, and Nathan and Grace sit in the back with me. Mom said she doesn't do funerals, which just made me want to scream. But that's not even the thing I'm most upset about right now. I can't believe Tucker left. He's visited his mom a few times since he moved out here, but he never took his guitar with him; he was always planning on coming back. He didn't even say goodbye.

I don't think he's going to come back this time, and each time I think that, my heart shatters into a million pieces. We weren't supposed to only have part of forever—he made me feel like we would last forever. It wasn't supposed to be like this. As mad as I am at him for leaving, I'm more upset with myself for lying. The whole reason he's gone is because I lied.

My stomach rolls when we pull up to the church where Lucy's funeral is being held. I remind myself to breathe, that maybe breathing will help the tight knot in my chest ease, but it does nothing to take away the feeling that I'm about to be swallowed whole.

"It's going to be okay," Grace says as she tugs me out of the car. "We'll be right here, and we can walk out at any point if you need to."

I let out a laugh, even though nothing about this is actually funny. "You can't walk out of a funeral."

Grace holds her head high as she loops her arm in mine. "Of course you can, especially when your friend just died of cancer and you also have cancer. That'd be a lot for anyone. So, we don't have to stay. If you need out, we'll walk out with you." I smile weakly at her. There is no way I'm leaving early.

"We can leave whenever you need to, Rosebud," Dad says, giving my shoulder a squeeze. I'm glad he came, but I won't leave early. We'll see this through.

My determination wavers when we enter the foyer and are surrounded by pictures of Lucy—a lot of them from when she was younger, but also a few recent ones, with her buzzed head and smiling face. Nathan grabs a program and we follow a line of people to a room in the back of the church for the viewing.

I stop abruptly. "I forgot we have to do this part," I say.

"We can just go to the chapel," Nathan offers, but I shake my head. Just because it's been a while since I've been to a funeral and just because I have cancer, too, doesn't mean I can't do this.

"It's okay, I'm okay, I just forgot. It's been a while since Grandma died." She was the last person I knew who passed away.

"You sure?" Nathan asks, and I nod, even though I'm not sure at all.

We enter the small room, and the casket is up against one wall, but we're far enough away that I can't see her yet. There's a line of people, including a few little kids, and I realize they must be Lucy's younger siblings. Her mom is at the very end of the line, so we say hello to all of the kids first, who look sad, but also a little bored.

"Hi," I say nervously to the woman who let her oldest daughter stay alone in the hospital week after week. I feel an anger I didn't know I felt bubble up in my chest.

"You must be Rosie," the woman says, and my heart softens just a little. Her face is puffy, like she's been crying as much as I have. "Luce told me so much about you."

Then she gives me a hug that I'm not quite ready for.

"Uh, yeah. I'm Rosie," I say as she pulls me to her chest. She smells like oranges and flowers.

"It's good to meet you," she says when she finally releases me. "Lucy would have been so glad you made it. I know she wanted us to meet before this, but here we are." She says it somewhat lightly, but I can hear the pain in her voice.

"I'm glad I'm here," I say, surprised at how honest the words feel. "Lucy was a good friend."

Lucy's mom's eyes water and I realize I still don't know her name. "Well, say a goodbye to her if you want; we'll see you in the chapel," she says. I nod and step back from her. Grace links my arm in hers again, and Nathan is close by. I am so grateful they didn't leave me alone for this.

I bite my lip as we approach the casket. It's Lucy, but it also doesn't look like Lucy. She was always so bright and bubbly and full of life, and I expect her to wake up and smile and tell me about the weather, or something equally as mundane, but with a huge smile on her face. My heart cracks when I remember that she won't ever do that again.

"We can go," I whisper to Grace, who has to pull me from the spot, as my feet seem to be glued to the ground.

I blink back tears as we walk into the chapel and sit down. I will not cry yet; maybe once people start talking and more people cry, but I will not cry yet. Grace keeps her arm linked with mine and Nathan takes my other hand; they might not know it, but they're anchoring me to reality, even though part of me desperately wants to run away. I know I won't leave; even if it's hard to be here, I can't leave. Lucy wouldn't leave and I want to be here for her, even though she's already gone.

The service is beautiful, but also a bit of a blur. My mind wanders to the tumor growing in my body, to the Paris Academy that still doesn't know my cancer is back, and to Tucker, more times than I'd like to admit. If I die, will he come to my funeral?

We sing songs of hope and grace, and Lucy's pastor speaks about life, peace, and life after death. I don't know if I believe any of it, but he has a soothing voice, and by the time he's done talking, I do feel a little calmer. Or maybe I'm just still numb.

We follow the long train of cars to the gravesite, since Lucy's parents said that Lucy wanted me to be there. I stand in the background of the family, not wanting to interrupt. One of Lucy's brothers, who looks about seventeen and has her same smile, reads a poem while he rests one hand on the closed casket. He doesn't cry, but many of the people who are here do, and when he's finished, he tucks the poem into one of the seams of the casket, as if the poem can rest with Lucy.

When it's all over, Lucy's mother invites us for food, but Dad tells her that I need to get home and rest because of the cancer. That makes Lucy's mom cry a little as she hugs me again, and she says to let her know if there's anything she can do for me.

"Well," I say, suddenly exhausted and grateful that Dad declined the offer for food.

"Let's get you home, Sis," Nathan says, leading me to the car. "You look like you need a nap."

"I don't think I've ever felt so drained in my life," I admit, and Grace just hugs my arm.

"Completely understandable," she says, and she holds my hand the entire ride home.

27

DOCTOR BARKER SAYS I have to start chemo almost immediately. There are more tests to take, and I have to get a port, but I'll be starting chemo in three days.

She said that at best, the chemo will shrink the tumor and put off surgery for a little longer. At worst, it will only give me a little extra time. It's not the best treatment, but there isn't really a 'best treatment' for where I have a tumor growing. Make it smaller, try surgery—that's the solution.

Deep down, I have the feeling that it won't work. I have a lot of regrets about how I've lived my life, especially this past year, but every time I think about how I could have been with Tucker the whole time, or told him the truth from the beginning, I push it away. It's too much to deal with right now.

I look at my phone, staring at the last text Tucker sent me; it was two days after he left, the morning of the funeral. I didn't tell anyone that he'd sent it to me.

TUCKER

I'm sorry, Rosie. I do love you so much (listen to In Case You Didn't Know by Brett Young). I do. I just… I'm sorry.

I didn't respond. I didn't know what to say. If you love someone, do you really walk away from them?

"Hey, Rosebud." Dad knocks on my door as he pushes it open and steps into my room. I set my phone down.

"Hi, Dad," I say.

"How are you feeling?" he asks, and I shrug, because even though I now know I have a tumor growing in my body, I feel the same way I did before.

Perfectly healthy. Well, almost perfectly healthy—I am a little more tired than usual.

How can you feel like you're completely fine while your body is essentially eating you from the inside out?

"I'm okay," I tell him, because even though I feel fine physically, I'm a little shaken up. Tucker's still gone, and Lucy is in the ground; how am I supposed to feel?

"Want to go to the studio today?" Dad asks, and it makes me smile.

"Yeah, I'd really like that." I get up and follow him out to the car. We don't talk about the cancer or about how I won't be going to Paris. Every time I think about that now, I cry.

My one and only dream, shattered.

We don't talk about how I'm going to lose my hair or about how after I start chemo, I might not be able to dance at all. Or about Mom, and how she's barely talked to me since the news of the new tumor, and when she does, she talks as if Paris will still happen. Just yesterday she told me that she made a new plan with Marie to help me get back on my feet after chemo. I wanted to tell her no, but she walked away before I got the chance. Even when I'm sick, it's always her way; she never asks what I might want.

Dad and I mostly sit in silence as we drive to the studio. He unlocks the door. It's Sunday, so there are no classes today. It'll just be us.

"I'll be waiting in Room 3," Dad says, and I walk back to the changing room alone. I change into my leotard and slip my pointe shoes on, pushing back the tears.

"This is not the last time," I whisper to myself. It can't be the last time. I will fight the cancer with everything I've got. I will dance until I physically can't, and then I'll fight some more, so that I can dance again.

"Whew," I let out a loud exhale and head to the practice room Dad's waiting in. It feels good to be here, to be dressed and have my pointe shoes laced up. I'm going to dance again.

He's sitting on a chair by the stereo. "You ready?" he asks and I nod. He pushes play.

I didn't have to ask which routine he'd pick. I already knew. I feel the familiar beat of my audition routine as the music fills the room, and for a moment, I let everything else fall away.

When I'm dancing, it's like nothing else exists beyond me and the music. As I leap across the floor, I feel my heart bursting. *This* is it. *This* is what I live for, what I'll keep living for.

When the song ends, I catch a glimpse of myself in the mirror. My face is covered with tears. I didn't even realize I'd been crying. I move to wipe them away, but Dad is there first. He brushes a thumb across my cheek, just like he did when I was a little girl, and then pulls me to him.

I can't tell if he's crying or not, but I don't want to let go. He has always been my anchor, and to see him break because of my diagnosis would kill me.

So, we stand there, hugging, for minutes or maybe hours, until Mom's voice breaks us apart.

"I figured you'd be here," she says and I pull away from Dad. My tears are gone now, and my eyes narrow into slits at the look on her face. She's been distant since we got the news, colder than usual, and I'm tired of it.

"I needed to dance before I get my port tomorrow and then start chemo," I tell her, even though I know I owe her no explanation. I am her daughter. I have cancer. I wanted to dance. She knows all that.

"Do it again," she says, her eyes never leaving mine.

"Catherine," Dad starts, but she holds up a hand to silence him.

"Do it again," she repeats. "We'll do it every day that the doctor says you're able, so you can still go to Paris."

"Catherine," Dad says again, but her eyes still don't leave mine.

"No," I say, possibly for the first time ever in response to my mom asking me to dance. I just danced for me, and it felt better than anything. But I'm not going to dance for her, not anymore.

The word takes her by surprise. "What do you mean, *no?*"

"I mean no," I say, standing up a little taller and lifting my chin to gaze at her. "I won't do it again."

"Why not?"

"I'm not going to Paris." I lose a little of my edge and my shoulders droop slightly, but I won't back down. "I have an inoperable tumor growing on my spinal cord. I'm sick."

"I know that." Her tone implies I've offended her.

"I don't think I'm going to get better."

Dad lets out a slow breath, but she ignores him.

"Do it again, Rosie," she says.

I shake my head. "Paris is all I've thought about for years and years. It's the only thing you've ever wanted for me, just because it didn't work out for you the way you wanted it to."

"Rosie," she warns, but I can't stop now—I have to say what I'm feeling, even though I didn't know I felt this way until now.

"You pushed me to be the best. I gave up everything to be the best. And for what? To die at eighteen?"

"You're not going to die," she says, her voice sharp.

"You don't know that." My voice gets a little louder and I shake my head again, throwing my hands up in the air. "I love ballet, I love it. But I let it consume me."

"And it was worth it—you got into the Paris Ballet Academy," she says, as if she's won.

"I lost Tucker because of it," I say. "And I nearly lost Grace."

"You lost them because you lied. Plus, you're better off without that boy."

"I lied because I thought I had to protect my future, to protect the opportunity to get into Paris! You never said it, but you were the only one who never told me to tell them the truth. Why? Because you knew that if anyone got a whiff of what was going on, my career would be over."

"You're being silly, darling," she says with false brightness. "You lied because you wanted to, not because of me."

"I did lie"—I clench my fists at my side—"but I did it because I knew what you'd say if I told them. I tried to date Shawn for months when I really wanted to be with Tucker, all because of you and what you'd think."

"He's not the kind of boy you want to love," she says. The stiffness in her voice is back. "He would only have distracted you."

"Just like Dad distracted you?" I don't want to hurt him, but I feel him flinch beside me. Mom glares.

"You know I love your father," she hisses at me like he's not standing right beside us. "He's the best part of my life."

"Then why are you still trying so hard to get me to the Paris Ballet Academy?" I ask, and something in her seems to crack. She takes a step back.

"You have to go." She's quieter now. Still angry, but quieter.

"I called them this morning," I say, surprising them both.

"You what?" Dad startles.

I look at him. "I called them to say that I have a highly progressed form of cancer and that I won't be attending in the fall."

"You. Did. Not." My mom says each word slowly.

"I did." I'm still looking at my dad. "And it really sucked, because even though Mom did push me so hard to get to Paris, it was my dream, too. I wanted to go, and now I can't."

My voice doesn't crack like I think it will as I say this. Instead, I feel strong for finally getting the words out.

"I'm ready to go home now," I tell Dad and he gives me a nod. Mom is still frozen to her spot. "Let me get my stuff from the locker room."

When I come back, Dad's holding Mom, and her shoulders are shaking. I don't know the reason for her tears—it could be because of something I said or because of my diagnosis. Either way, I don't regret what I said. I don't regret standing up to her and telling her no.

That last runthrough was perfect. I may never dance that routine again, but now I don't have to, because I did it one last time, on my terms.

28

THE BRIGHT SUN peeking through the blinds in my room makes me blink as I open my eyes. I've spent the past three weeks in this room, getting poison pumped into my body. Yesterday was my last round of chemo before Doctor Barker will see if it's working and if the tumor has gotten any smaller.

My room is quiet—Dad's asleep on the couch and I can see Nathan and Grace in the hallway. *Where's Tucker?* I want to ask, *have you heard from him?* But no one even knows I'm awake yet.

My head is throbbing, but other than that, I feel almost completely normal. "Dad," I whisper, and his eyes fly open.

"Hey, Rosebud." He leans over me, touching my cheek, and I lean into his hand.

After he helps me drink some water, Nathan and Grace come into my room. Grace won't meet my eye, and Nathan looks sad.

"What's going on?" I ask. I want to know why everyone seems so solemn. Mom enters the room, followed by Doctor Barker.

"You're up," Doctor Barker says, in a way that reminds me far too much of Lucy, and my stomach clenches.

"Yeah?" I ask. Why wouldn't I be up?

"You've been asleep for almost three days," Doctor Barker explains, and I look at her, confused.

"But, chemo..." I start, and then I remember. I remember getting chemo started, and everything feeling heavy and dark.

"What do you remember?" Mom asks quietly.

"It was dark..." I offer and Doctor Barker nods.

"You had a seizure in the middle of your last round of chemo. We had to sedate you to make it stop," Doctor Barker says. "But, once your brain activity was normal, we took you off those meds, and now you're awake."

I nod. It's a lot to take in. This feels too soon, too sudden. I knew Lucy had seizures, but I never asked her when they started. Maybe she had them the whole time they'd known about the tumor, and not just at the end. Or maybe they were only at the end and I have less time than we originally thought.

Mom gives me a small smile. "They're going to keep you here for a few more days, but things are looking good." Things are still tense between us, but I can tell she's trying. We might never be okay, her and I, but maybe things can get better. But, after that day in the studio when I saw her crying, things have been a little different.

"Well, not good, exactly," Doctor Barker corrects and we all look at her. "Your tumor hasn't gotten any bigger, but it also hasn't gotten smaller."

"We didn't know if that would happen though, right?"

Doctor Barker shakes her head.

I think part of me knew from the moment I heard the cancer was back that this would be a losing battle; one that I was willing to fight, but one that my body wouldn't win.

I swallow. I ask the question I know everyone is thinking, "How long?"

"Still hard to say. If we continue to do chemo, we can keep the tumor from growing, but we can't do that forever. There will be a time when the chemo and the side effects aren't worth it, and there won't be much time after that, I'm afraid," Doctor Barker says. The words zip through me, as if I was just struck by lightning, but no one else moves. They already knew.

"How did it get this bad?" I whisper.

"Sometimes these things just happen," Doctor Barker says, sadly. She lets my dad know she'll be back to check on me, but that I should rest if I can.

If I can. I just found out I don't have much life left. How can I rest?

"Any word from Tucker?" I finally ask. It's as if the room fills with ice—no one moves or talks. "Can I have my phone to call him?" I ask this question to Nathan, since he's been in charge of my phone while I've been at the hospital.

Grace comes to the other side of my bed, her eyes full of tears. "I've tried, his cell must be off."

My heart clenches. "Any word from his mom?" Grace reached out to her as soon as Tucker left.

"We haven't heard from her either," she says.

"Can I still try to call him?" I ask, and Nathan hands me my phone. I hit Tucker's name but it goes straight to voicemail. "Um, hi," I say into the phone. "Things aren't great over here, um, with the cancer, I mean. Not that I'm doing great either. I, uh, come home, please? I need you here." I hang up and sink back into my pillows.

"That was not the best message," Nathan says jokingly.

"I..." I begin, and then I start to laugh, too. "Apparently I can't talk right now." That seems to be all that everyone else needed, because then we're all laughing.

"Why are we laughing?" Nathan asks, wiping away his tears.

"Maybe we're all just in denial?" Grace offers.

"Or maybe it's like in *Grey's Anatomy*, when they're at the funeral and everyone can't stop laughing, even though it's a totally inappropriate time to be laughing," Dad says from the corner, which for some reason makes us all laugh harder.

When the laughter finally runs down, I ask, "Maybe he went to the cabin?" Tucker has to be somewhere.

"My dad checked on Monday and it was empty. He's going to go up again tomorrow," Grace tells me.

"He was worried that he's like his dad," I say suddenly.

"What?" she asks.

"Once, he told me that one of his fears is that he'd just grow up and walk away from the people he loved, just like his dad. That music would become so much of his life, he'd walk away from everything else. He was worried he had the running gene in him," I say, and the words feel heavy on my tongue.

"He's not like his dad," she assures me. "Get some sleep, we'll find him."

"You get to go home," Doctor Barker announces.

Mom bursts into tears and Grace collapses on the bed beside me and says, "Thank you, God."

I'm glad I'm going home. It'll be nice to be in a place that isn't this white, sterile room, surrounded by all the beeping, though Doctor Barker assures Mom that some of the equipment will be coming with me so the nurses who are coming home with us will be able to monitor me.

This isn't the end—not yet—but the end feels suffocatingly close.

And we still have no idea where Tucker is.

I fall asleep before the conversation is over.

letter to tucker

DEAR TUCKER,

    I had to write you another letter because you won't answer my calls and I need to tell you a few things.

    Again, I need to say that I'm sorry. For not being with you and loving you sooner. For getting sick; I know that's a lot to handle. I don't blame you for leaving, but I still hate that you did.

    My cancer is bad. I'm home now, with a nurse that comes over a lot, and not officially on hospice, but that's kind of what it feels like. And while no one says it, that's where this is headed. Whether it's next week or even a year from now... Basically, I just get to stay home instead of living at the hospital like Lucy did. It's kind of insane how quickly I went from feeling fine to feeling so sick all the time. That's where I'm at right now, sick and weak. And I've got headaches nearly all the time. I'm not really sure how Lucy was so happy all the time if she felt anything like this. I'm grouchy and snap at everyone, so while I hate that you aren't here, I'm glad you don't have to see me like this.

    I also wanted to talk about something other than cancer. Back to the whole soulmates thing from my last letter. Because I've been thinking about this a lot. About how maybe for this moment in time, you got to be mine and I got to be yours. And if soulmates are a thing, I think you're mine.

This letter isn't a goodbye, but I guess it also sort of is, because I don't know if you'll ever come back. Which is breaking me into a million little pieces.

I was talking to Dad about this right before we left the hospital, and he said a few things that I need to share.

Maybe we're only destined to have one soulmate, or maybe we get more than one in our lifetime. But if you find that person (or persons), the one that looks at you like you're the sun and moon and stars, hang on. Love them deeply and tell them again and again how you feel. Don't walk away if you don't have to. Because life is too short to live with regrets and to live without the one your soul longs to be with. So, take the leap, say the words, and dream big.

Because in the end, you'll be glad you did.

So, this is me saying the words. I love you, Tucker. I love you so much that it hurts. I didn't know that you could find your soulmate at eighteen. I don't know if that's what we are—all I know is that something has always drawn me to you, and that you'll be in my heart, always.

I also want to say that I believe in you. You're going to do great things and write great music and change so many lives with your songs. So please, please, please don't give up. Even when things are hard. Keep going, keep trying. Keep thinking of me and hanging onto my belief in you. Because you are already a rockstar—you're my rockstar, and I can't wait to cheer you on from the stars.

I love you. I always will. And I just needed you to know that.

Love you always,

Rosie

29

I'VE OFFICIALLY BEEN HOME for three days, and when I wake up, Grace shakes her head the moment I open my eyes. "Still no word," she says, shoulders slumped. We're all camped out in the family room. Mom and Dad are watching *You've Got Mail*, Nathan is painting my toenails, and Grace sits next to me with my phone in one hand and hers in the other.

It's officially summer break and I missed graduation. Even though I'm not dying right this second, everyone doesn't want to be too far away from me at any given moment—not that I mind the company. This is the most time I've ever seen Mom take away from the studio.

But it's obvious that someone is missing.

He'll come back, I think to myself. *I know he'll come back.* I know Tucker, and I know that he'll be back.

I shift, moving myself into a sitting position. I'm not great, but I'm okay.

The shadows stretching across the wall tell me that the sun is about to set. I offer Grace and Nathan a smile as I look around the room. I guess if I'm dying, this is a good place to be, surrounded by people who I love and who love me. Doctor Barker said it might not be like this always, that my body is still recovering from the chemo and that I will probably be able to do pretty normal things for a little while, especially if I do another round of chemo. I'm still waiting to hear if the tumor is still the same size.

But even if it hasn't grown, it feels close to the end.

"Hey, Dad," I say, startling nearly everyone in the room. They go back to their activities and he makes his way over to me.

"Yes, Rosebud?" he asks, sitting down beside me.

"I think I get it now," I tell him.

He takes my hand. "Get what, sweetheart?"

"Why things like this happen."

"If you have that answer, I'd love to know," he says with a smile, but I can see the pain and heartache in his eyes.

I smile at him. "Okay, so maybe I don't know, but I think I get it. Or at least, I understand what you said. That sometimes we have to go through stuff even if it's hard, so that we can become better."

"Yeah?"

"Yeah," I say. "I'm still not sure there's a God or a heaven, but I hope so. I hope I'll get to see Lucy, and then I can ask God why He gave us both cancer and why we both had to die so young."

Dad wipes away a tear with the back of his hand, but I'm strangely not emotional.

"So maybe I don't get it exactly, but I'd like to believe that maybe He is up there. That maybe all of this had a reason. Like I had to learn that I wasn't only supposed to be focused on dance. Or maybe that dance could still matter, but that the people around me matter more. I think Lucy said something like that the first time I met her, and I'm pretty sure I didn't believe her... but I do now."

"I'm glad, sweetheart," he says, his eyes watery. "I'm sorry that Tucker hasn't come back."

Every time I think about Tucker, it feels like I've had the wind knocked out of me. It's almost always impossible to breathe when I think of him.

"He'll come back," I say, even though with each passing day, I don't know if I believe it anymore. "He'll come back."

"I hope so," Dad says, and we both watch the movie playing on the TV, even though I don't think either of us are actually paying attention.

It's a few hours later when the front door opens quietly, and everyone perks up as Tucker enters the room, followed by his mom, who I've only seen in pictures. If I could, I'd get up and run to him right now. Instead, he's by my side in seconds.

He is back.

"I'm so sorry," he says, over and over, as he takes me in his arms and pulls me onto his lap. "I'm so sorry."

"Where were you?" I whisper. Nathan tugs on Grace's sleeve to give us some room, and even my parents head into the kitchen, talking with Tucker's mom.

"I was headed for Nashville." He pulls away from me slightly, so he can look in my eyes. "I turned off my phone and just started driving."

"You're not your dad," I tell him.

He nods, but he looks guilty.

"I just, I'm so sorry, Rosie." He presses his head against mine. "I was just so overwhelmed, I thought I couldn't do it anymore. I didn't want you to die, and I freaked out, and thought that leaving might be the best option, so I ran, and then I really felt like I was my dad."

"You can't run," I tell him, "when things get hard. Running is not the answer."

He nods. "I know, and I'm so sorry."

"What day is it?" I ask him. I've lost all track of time since I got home.

"First Saturday in June," he tells me. He's been gone for five weeks. "I made it to Utah and I decided to charge my phone. There were so many missed calls, and that's when I noticed Mom had called about a hundred times."

Bless his mom's heart. "And?"

"And I ignored her. Even when she told me she was coming out to California, and I started my way back. I still wasn't ready." He looks down, ashamed. "I went to my grandparents' cabin, which wasn't the best idea, because all I could think about was you and our almost perfect night."

"You took your guitar," I murmur. For some reason, this is the part that stings the most. It hurts that he left, that he walked away from me, from us. But knowing he took his guitar made it more real. I'd hoped he would come back, but there was no guarantee, because he took the only thing he loves as much as me.

"I know," he says, knowing exactly what that made me think and feel. That he was going to be gone for good. "I wasn't planning on coming back." He runs a hand through his hair. "I'm sorry, Rosie. I've been working with Murphy in LA, trying to get my set ready for opening with Peyton, but that's not going well. And yesterday, I headed up to the cabin, and I got a text from Mom telling me she was coming." He cradles my face in his hands. "I didn't want to leave. I got scared. I wanted a new life, even if it was just for a day. But then as the days passed, well, I realized that life isn't life without you in it. And even though, well," he says all of this in a rush and then lets out a small sob, "even though I don't get forever with you, at least we got some time."

I nod, because that's exactly how I feel. If I could do life over again, I'd choose to be with him sooner, but even if I couldn't do that, I won't ever regret a second that I spent with him.

"I wrote you a song," he says, then he gently sets me back on my makeshift bed and grabs his guitar from the hallway.

"I thought you said you've been struggling with music?" I ask, confused.

"Yeah, but the words just came the other day while I was sitting in my hotel room, and the chords came yesterday at the cabin." He settles on the bed in front of me, his guitar in his lap. It reminds me of the first time he played for me, all those months ago, when we were still just flirting and everything was new and happy.

He closes his eyes and starts to play. I watch his face and he looks more relaxed than when he left. Whatever happened to him on his runaway trip changed him.

Then he starts singing, and I remember all the reasons I fell in love with him in the first place. I close my eyes and listen to the music and the words as he sings.

They say eighteen's too young to know
'Bout how to feel and how to show it
But that never was a problem for me,
Like that ol' song says, I got my eyes on you
And there ain't nothing I'd rather do
Than be yours forever

Sometimes life don't go as planned
Sometimes life makes you so damn mad
But I got you
Yeah I got you, I got you
For part of forever
Yeah I got you, I got you, I got you
For part of forever.

I see that old picture of us
Wondering if you'd ever know
We were meant to be, just like that
Spent the last six months lovin' you

And there ain't nothing I'd rather do
Than be yours forever

Sometimes life don't go as planned
Sometimes life makes you so damn sad
But I got you
Yeah I got you, I got you
For part of forever
Yeah I got you, I got you, I got you
For part of forever.

We're both quiet for a minute after he stops singing. He leans over and gently presses his lips to mine. "I know it's not quite finished yet, but I love you, Rosie," he says before kissing me again. "I'll always love you."

"I love you too," I whisper, because talking is hard. He holds me and everyone returns from the kitchen. He adjusts so I'm leaning against him, his arms around me.

"I would have killed you if you didn't come back." Grace smacks one of Tucker's arms.

"I know." Tucker kisses my temple and pulls me closer to him. "I would have killed me, too."

"I still might," she threatens, and my eyes droop.

Nathan lies down with his head in my lap, and Grace holds one of my hands while Mom settles in next to Nathan. Everyone's quiet as the last few minutes of *You've Got Mail* plays on the TV.

Tucker whispers in my ear, telling me all about the life he dreamed of for us. The life I'll fall asleep dreaming about. I'm in and out of sleep all night.

The morning sun fills the room and I'm surrounded by all of my favorite people. I don't know what the day will bring, but I do know that every day after this, the sun will continue to rise. Even when life doesn't go as planned, it keeps on going, and most of us keep on living. And if we're going to live, we may as well do the things we want now, because we never know how much time we have. We should say I love you, and chase our dreams. We should take risks, and do it now, because tomorrow might be too late.

"I love you, darlin'," Tucker says as he presses his lips into my hair.

"Love you always," I whisper back.

after - letter from tucker to rosie

Dear Rosie,

It's been exactly two years since you silently slipped away in your sleep. You were in my arms, and Grace, Nathan, your parents, Erin, and the twins, were all crowded in your bedroom. You fought a good fight against your cancer and I'm so glad we got the time that we did together.

After that day, I didn't know how to go on, for so long. What they say about grief is true, that it comes in waves. At first it felt like I was getting pulled under by a tsunami, but slowly, it started to ebb a little more. About a year after you died, I was doing an interview for Nash Country Weekly. It's not The Rolling Stones, but it's something! Grace says that you know, that you're somewhere up there watching everything that's happening. I really hope that's true.

But I guess I should back up a little bit. The week after you died, I got a call from Murphy. I told her that, no, there was no way I'd be able to go on tour with Peyton (for the second time) that fall after losing you. We'd done it the year before, and you were at every show in California that you were well enough to be at, despite the chemo making you so sick and the tumor by your brain sometimes making

"

you have seizures. But you were there. You got better for a little while, after things got bad after graduation. You were doing okay, until you weren't.

The next year, she wanted me to open for her again, but I was drowning with the loss of you. There was no way I'd be able to go and tour now that you were gone. How was I supposed to live my life without you? How am I supposed to live my life without you? You were—are—my everything. There was no way I'd be able to sing. Thankfully, Murphy knew what was going on, and didn't tell Peyton that I'd said no.

The day before Murphy called again, Nathan showed up with a box he'd found while they were going through your room. It was pink and your dad painted a ballerina on it when you were little. Inside the box was a journal and some letters from you. Nathan and I talked for a while; he's doing good. Still dating Grace and he's going to school to be a doctor, in hopes of helping more kids with cancer some day.

I mentioned how when you fall in love for the first time, there's this part of you that thinks 'this is it' and not in a way that makes you feel stuck or trapped, but in a way that gives you even more butterflies than before. Like you didn't know it was possible to care about someone that much, but now you do, and you can't imagine life without them. That's how it felt falling in love with you, Rosie. And Nathan agreed that the love we had, it was something special.

I was head over heels (can a guy say that?) and I didn't care who knew it. I felt all those feelings come rushing back as I read those letters from you. It was as if I was right there, back at the beginning again, only this time I was seeing it all from your eyes and I loved that. I thought we were forever, Rosie. I wanted us to be forever, but we don't always get what we want.

At least, not everything we want.

When Murphy called the next day, asking again if I wanted to open for Peyton, I said I'd do it, but only if they'd let me have a moment of silence at each concert in honor of you. Turns out Peyton is also a hopeless romantic and thought it was sweet. Needless to say, that tour kicked off my music career.

Last year, my first album, ROSIE, was about to come out, and that's when I had the interview. I still felt so heavy that you weren't here to see it all happen, that you weren't here to live your dreams. In the interview, you came up. That's what happens when you name your album after a girl.

"So, who's this Rosie?" the journalist asked me. "And when do we get to meet her?"

My heart dropped, just like it always does when someone asks me this question. I don't get the second one as often; if anyone was at any of the shows on tour the fall before, they know who you are and why I choose to honor you. This journalist though, either didn't know, or she didn't care.

"Rosie is the love of my life," I told her, "but she's been gone for about a year now, cancer."

The journalist's eyes flickered in surprise, so she didn't know. Which sort of made me want to laugh—I mean, for her, I was just an assignment.

"I'm so sorry," she said. "How did you keep going, after her loss?"

Then I just started talking. I didn't know I believed the words I was saying until I said them. "Some days I feel like I can't breathe, I get so sad that Rosie isn't here to see this, that she's not here for me to love, that she doesn't get to live her own dreams, because she was taken way too soon. But I'm the man I am today because of her.

"Not because she died, but because of her love. Loving Rosie was all-consuming, but in the very best way. When she loved something or someone, she gave it her whole heart. She had a way of filling you up. And even at the end, when she was so sick, seeing her still made the day better.

"Loving her made me who I am. And because I love her, I get up and I sing. She would have killed me if I sat on my bed and stopped living my life after she died. I mean, I did do that for a while, but then I realized that the ache of missing her might always be there,

that because of who she was to me, the heartache might not ever go away, not that I'd ever really want it to. But I realized I could either crumble, or I could rise and make her proud, and that's what I chose to do."

Like I said earlier, I thought that you were my forever, Rosie. But I'm just so glad that we got part of forever together.

I love you. I miss you.

Today I'm going to leave pink and yellow tulips on your grave. Then I'm going out with your parents, Nathan, and Grace to get some fish tacos at that food truck you love. Cause we all know that's what you would have wanted. Next week, I start my very first tour, all on my own. I know you'll be there with me, at every show.

I don't really know how to end this letter, but I guess I'll say this: I hope you're proud of me. I'm trying, I'm living, and I think that's all I really can do, because I miss you like crazy.

You were the best part of my life and nothing will ever change that.

I love you, Rosie, I always will. I hope you're dancing up there in heaven. Save a dance for me.

Love you always,
Tucker

acknowledgments

I don't know where to begin with this book. There are so many people I need and want to thank. I started writing this book when I was in the depths of post-partum depression back in 2019. Rosie and Tucker gave me something outside of myself to live for, and I'll be forever grateful to them. Their story changed a lot from that first draft to this one, but I've loved every minute I've got to spend with them, so yeah, I've got to thank them first.

For my original beta readers (in like 2020), Ashley N., Erica, Alexis, Grace, Becca, McKenna, and Ashley W., THANK YOU!

Thank you to all of my Kickstarter supporters. It was so fun to get this book out to you before publishing it anywhere else. Thank you for backing the project and helping me cover some of the publishing expenses.

To my parents, who always encourage me, my daughter, who always asks me if I'm writing another book, and my ever-supportive husband, thank you, thank you, thank you.

about the author

Taylor Epperson has dreamed of writing books since she was a kid. She firmly believes that every story needs kissing and romance. Her stories will make you swoon, laugh, and maybe cry. But hopefully they'll always leave you feeling a little happier.

When she's not writing, you can find her curled up with a good book and a bag of potato chips or playing with her daughter. She enjoys binge-watching cooking shows and crime dramas. She lives in Northern Colorado with her husband, daughter, two hilarious cats, and one black lab.

also by taylor epperson

If you loved this book, you will love Taylor's other books.

The Nelson Sisters Series

The Luck of Finding You

The Rules of Mistletoe (Holly & Drew)

Begin Again (Annie & Sam)

Sunkissed Summer Novella

Off Trail Love (Jack & Maggie)

Poetry

In Which I Try to Save the World

Starlight Springs

Only a Game (Coming in 2026)

A SUNKISSED SUMMER NOVELLA

Off Trail
Love

TAYLOR EPPERSON

TAYLOR EPPERSON

the Luck of Finding you

TAYLOR EPPERSON

the Rules of Mistletoe

TAYLOR EPPERSON
begin again
the WEDNESDAY CAFE
open

www.ingramcontent.com/pod-product-compliance
Lightning Source LLC
Chambersburg PA
CBHW032248310726
48973CB00008B/2344